THE GRA

Charlotte Bush, who was so beautiful that all of us in the sixth form were wild about her, was sitting in front of me in the lecture theatre when the picture was flashed onto the screen. I could see she didn't believe it. Nor did I. It showed a grasshopper much larger than a man. But there was something else about it that excited her— something that her boyfriend, Harry Green, knew more about, but wasn't saying. Even Charlotte couldn't make him reveal all he knew.

There was a big gap between Harry and Charlotte on Weldelph's social ladder, she was near the bottom rung and he was the only son of one of the town's wealthiest families, and it got far worse when an older man, Hugh Beamish, couldn't resist the charms of Charlotte, the beautiful schoolgirl. I was drawn into the whirlpool that this caused as an even greater scandal broke over Weldelph.

And at the centre of it all was that mysterious grass-hopper . . .

THE GRASSHOPPER

John Gordon

THE BODLEY HEAD
LONDON

British Library Cataloguing
in Publication Data
Gordon, John
The grasshopper.
I. Title
823'.914[F] PR6057.06/
ISBN 0-370-31159-0

© John Gordon 1987
Printed in Great Britain for
The Bodley Head Ltd
32 Bedford Square, London WC1B 3EL
by Cox & Wyman
First published in Great Britain 1987

For Sally and Viddi

Contents

PART ONE

1 The Weldelph Scandal

Everybody by now has heard of the Weldelph Scandal, but only a very few know what really happened, and they aren't likely to talk. But I think it ought to be written down, so that's what I'm going to do before everybody's memory fades. My words are a time trap.

It began in a very unlikely way—with a lecture in a museum. The lecturer was Hugh Beamish, who was the brand new curator of the only museum in Weldelph. He was—still is, come to that—getting on for thirty so he was a good bit older than us. He was very dark and tall, and good-looking in a thin-faced, high-cheekboned sort of way, and he was clever but charming with it. He always looked full of himself, absolutely the guy in charge, but that was before all the disgrace came his way. Before the grasshopper got to work—and before he met Charlotte.

I myself hadn't been in Weldelph very long (my father had just changed his job, so we'd moved) and I hardly knew anybody when I saw Hugh Beamish for the first time. This was the night of the lecture. His subject was his 'First Impressions of Weldelph', and I only went along because I was like him, a newcomer. I'll admit I was a bit surprised to see in the audience two people I knew in the sixth form—at least I knew them by sight as I was still a bit of an outsider, so I didn't push myself forward but I got as close as I could and sat in the row behind them. One of them was Harry Green and the other was Charlotte—Charlotte Bush, and nobody who's seen her could ever blame Hugh Beamish for what happened.

It was a winter's night not long before Christmas and the lecture was averagely dull, although to judge by the way that Harry Green was fidgeting and sighing you might have thought he'd strayed into the long, dark room expecting it to be a disco. But it just might have been more than boredom that disturbed him, even at that stage. It could have been the first stirrings of jealousy, for Charlotte was hanging on to every word the lecturer uttered, as even I could see, and she was responsible for Harry being there in the first place. She had dragged him along against his will. But Charlotte could persuade anybody, any male, that is, to go anywhere with her. Harry was lucky to be chosen.

It was not until the lecture was almost over that Harry showed any interest whatever, and that was when Hugh Beamish rapped the floor with his lecturer's pointer and a new picture flashed onto the screen. When she saw it Charlotte gasped, and it certainly made Harry sit up. But at the same instant there was laughter from the audience, for what the picture showed was impossible.

'A fearsome beast,' said Hugh Beamish, playing up to his first laugh of the evening. 'A truly remarkable animal.'

But I was listening to Charlotte, who had swung her head towards Harry and was whispering excitedly. 'It's yours!' she said. 'The same picture you told me about!'

'Might be.' He had overcome his own excitement and now was staring impassively at the screen.

'There's no "might be" about it,' she said. 'It's the same grasshopper.'

Charlotte has a perfect profile, and I would have been content just to look at her silhouette against the screen if the picture had not been so strange. It did, in fact, show a grasshopper but, judging by the man who stood along-

10

side it in the picture, it was a grasshopper as large as a horse. It was a photograph and it must have been pretty old to go by the man's cropped hair and his heavy moustache, and it was enlarged to a cloudy graininess, but the insect really was very lifelike. The man, who was in waistcoat and shirtsleeves, appeared to have been riding it. He still held its reins. It was crazy.

'Can it be real?' Hugh Beamish's voice echoed in the long, high room. 'Do you breed insects like that out here in the fens?'

It was a feeble joke and it made Harry squirm. 'He's a nut case,' he said, and he slumped down in his seat.

Charlotte did not want him to retreat. 'Tell him,' she whispered. 'Tell him you know something about it.'

'Why should I?'

She didn't like that, and she sat back and just stared at him as he looked at the screen. I knew how he appeared to her at that moment. He was pug-faced and looked like a sulky kid. She was still staring at him when Hugh Beamish began to tell everybody his theory of what the picture really was.

'I discovered this awesome steed in a pile of unsorted papers in the archive,' he said. 'There was no note or inscription to say what it was, but I imagine it is an early example of trick photography.'

He paused for comment, but none came, although Charlotte, still exasperated by Harry, leant forward suddenly and caught Hugh Beamish's eye. 'Yes?' he said, expecting a question, but she shook her head. The damage, however, had been done. In the mysterious dimness of light reflected from the screen he had caught his first glimpse of Charlotte and in that moment his life lurched in a new direction. He didn't know it, but it's true. Her eyes, like two large dark commas, rested on him, and he gazed towards her for a full second longer than he need have done. Then he rapped the floor, and the grasshopper vanished.

11

'And this is the last picture I wish to show you,' he said. The screen now showed the fens around Weldelph, a low horizon and the setting sun in an empty sky. 'It is a landscape I have learned to love,' he lied. Hugh Beamish was a Devon man and I've heard him whicker on about pretty lanes and swelling hills, but that night he was flattering the natives. Not everybody, especially not everybody in Weldelph, fell for his sort of charm, and I must say I winced a bit myself when Mrs Frost, his assistant, cut him short, stumped across the floor and switched on the lights. The pale globes came on high overhead and made you think of the black winter sky beyond the windows—except for Hugh Beamish, that is. I saw his eyes seeking out the girl.

Charlotte, I knew, was less mysteriously beautiful than she had been in the dimness. Prettier, however. Hideously pretty for a man of his age, I expect, for now he could see that she was no more than a schoolgirl. He has since admitted that the badge on her breast pocket was a danger sign that should have warned him off.

The audience, apart from ourselves, was elderly, and even before the applause had died away Harry was on his feet. 'Let's get out of here,' he said.

But Charlotte tugged at his arm. 'Aren't we going to tell him?' she asked.

'About what?' He pretended ignorance, but not for long with those comma eyes on him. 'About that stupid bloody grasshopper, you mean? I don't know anything more about it than he does.'

'Oh yes, you do!'

'Well, he can find out for himself. He's got nothing else to do.'

It was quite a spat and they didn't shut up until Hugh Beamish began to come towards them. The library was emptying and Charlotte was shuffling into her coat. Hugh Beamish helped her. 'Thank you, Mr Beamish,' she said.

12

'*Hugh* Beamish,' he told her, and she blushed.

'Anyway we was just talking about you,' she said, and instantly went very red. Normally it doesn't matter when Charlotte's grammar slips into common Weldelph, because we all speak two tongues, but in front of this man it embarrassed her. He had very handsome vowels. 'We was . . .' It came again in spite of herself. 'We were just saying it was a good job we came tonight because you said a lot of stuff that's going to be useful for us, didn't we?' She looked towards Harry to back her, but he stood where he was with his head lowered and his hands jammed into his windcheater pockets. He was aggressive, definitely, but Hugh Beamish smiled. He had the moral advantage, after all.

'I fear I was fiendishly dull,' he said, 'and I completely fail to see how my first impressions of your delightful Fenland can be of the slightest *use* to anyone at all.'

'At school,' said Charlotte. 'Social studies. That's why we came to hear you.'

'How dreary,' said Beamish, but he kept smiling and it was possible to see he was calculating our ages, particularly Charlotte's, to gauge how he should behave towards us. 'Well, at least there was that fantastic grasshopper,' he said. 'Wasn't that quite an extraordinary thing to find?'

Harry glanced up. There was no mistaking the fact that Hugh Beamish, much older as he was, was displaying to a female. The curator gestured with his long arms, and his voice was full of status, a mixture of vowels both clipped and drawled. We heard 'fentestic' and 'extrawdinary'.

'Well,' said Charlotte, 'we know something about that grasshopper, don't we, Harry?'

I was as much in the dark as Hugh Beamish and was quite eager to have the picture explained, but Harry stood where he was, head bowed, and didn't say a word. My interest began to dwindle because the photograph

13

was an obvious fake, some sort of joke. But something about it had agitated Charlotte.

'Harry knows a man.' She spoke jerkily, caught between two antagonistic males and wanting to keep the peace. 'This man showed you a poster, didn't he, Harry?'

Harry had the decency to nod his blond head, but that was all.

'It was only a little poster,' said Charlotte, 'no bigger than that,' and her fingers sketched the size of a smallish sheet of paper, 'and it wasn't a photograph but it was a picture of a huge grasshopper, and it offered a reward. Five pounds, it said, for anybody who could ride it when it came to the Mart.'

'The what?' said Beamish, who was very much taken by her girlish gestures, which she only made because she was embarrassed.

'The Mart,' she said softly, not sure that it was a proper word.

Harry at last came to her rescue. 'It's a fair,' he said. 'Weldelph Mart is a fair and it comes round once a year.' I was on the fringes of their encounter, an observer rather than a participant, but I wondered if I would have to intervene because Harry's antagonism was so strong. He was shorter than Hugh Beamish, but he stood with his head thrust forward on his broad shoulders and he was formidable in his present mood. 'There's no grasshopper at the Mart nowadays, so I think you've had it.'

'Oh, I see,' said Beamish, still smiling. 'So it was some sort of fairground ride—a mule dressed up, or something of the kind. A bucking bronco sort of thing.'

'Could've been.'

Harry had turned and was already walking towards the foyer, but Charlotte lingered, afraid that he had offended the curator. Hugh Beamish, however, bowed and ushered her after Harry. I drifted along as well.

'Rather disappointing,' he said. 'I had hoped it was a genuine creature unknown to science.'

'It had a name,' said Charlotte. 'There was a name on the poster, wasn't there, Harry?' We had caught up with him by the front door. 'I can't remember what it was.'

'Cox's Animals,' Harry grunted, 'that's all. Doesn't mean a thing.'

Hugh Beamish, at the moment of parting, decided it was time to show that he was not cowed by Harry's behaviour. 'You may be mistaken there,' he said. 'Every scrap of evidence counts if we are to get to the bottom of this little mystery.'

Harry shrugged, dismissing it. I also hoped the matter would be dropped, but the new curator was not to be shaken off. 'This person who showed you the poster,' he said, 'would he produce it for me, do you think?'

'It was only junk,' said Harry. 'I should think he's burnt it by now.' He opened the door, hunching his shoulders and turning his back towards the rest of us. It was then that Hugh Beamish showed he was not an easy man to put down. He was so polite it was an insult.

'It's a great shame if it's been lost,' he said pleasantly. 'Nevertheless, many thanks for putting me in the picture, Harry.'

It would have been Harry's style, in his surly mood that moment, to shuffle off without another word, but quite suddenly he turned around and smiled. 'I like putting people in the pictuar,' he said. He emphasized every syllable of 'pict-you-are' and the odd pronunciation made all of us, except Hugh Beamish, laugh. He clearly thought that Harry was mocking his own cultivated drawl, but he did manage a sour little smile.

He was mistaken about Harry taking the juice. In fact, what Harry was doing was giving him a clue. He was telling him who owned the poster, and anybody except a newcomer to Weldelph would have known who he meant. I knew because everybody in the sixth knew it, but poor old Hugh Beamish was out in the cold. And Charlotte was sorry for him, I could see that, but before she had a chance to put it right Harry hurried her away.

When I had followed them down the steps into Ely Crescent I looked back at the entrance and saw Hugh Beamish gazing after us through the glass panels of the door. There were a good many years between us, but at that moment he seemed as lonely as a boy who had been left out of a game. It would have been better for several people, including himself, if he had never been allowed to join in.

2 'All You Have To Do Is Look'

Now that I knew, or thought I knew, where Harry had gleaned his knowledge of the strange grasshopper I was as keen as Charlotte to learn more, but I didn't get a chance to do it that night. Their passions were so high they ignored me altogether. I witnessed some of what happened next, but my direction lay elsewhere and I have had to piece together what took place from what they told me later when they each wanted a shoulder to cry on.

Charlotte barely waited for the museum door to close behind us before she rounded on Harry.

'You were pretty nasty,' she said. Harry's mouth opened, but she did not give him time to answer. 'And you know what I mean. You were nasty to *him*.' She nodded towards the door. 'He hasn't been here long, but that didn't seem to matter to you. You were really horrible to him.'

'I deny it.' Harry looked away. 'Anyway he deserved it. Lanky great twit.'

'Why? What has he ever done to you?'

16

'Nothing except bore the arse off me. Not that it was my arse he was after.'

'What's that supposed to mean?'

'Nothing,' he said. 'Nothing at all.'

A freezing wind cut into us as we stood at the foot of the steps, but Harry ignored it to look left and right along the two wings of Ely Crescent. The museum was at its centre, and the fronts of the houses, sharpened by moonlight, curved away like a sickle biting into the rushing air. Clouds, fringed in silver, raced overhead. 'Snow soon,' he said, but Charlotte was already walking away. He followed her, and turned his back to the wind to stride backwards in front of her. 'It's going to snow before long.'

'Why are you walking like that?'

'Because I'm backward.'

'That's exactly what you are.' She did not laugh.

'At least I see things different this way. And I don't have to screw my eyes up like you.' The wind parted his hair at the back and chilled his scalp like iced water, but he let it pour over him and tilted his face to the silver clouds. 'They look as if they're carrying messages somewhere,' he said, but she had her nose in her collar and paid him no attention.

There was a big gulf between Charlotte and Harry, and it wasn't just that her accent slipped more often than his. As a matter of fact, Harry was so many rungs above her on Weldelph's social ladder that he was practically out of reach, but there was more to it than that. They saw things differently. Harry was mad about pictures—which was why somebody had shown him the peculiar grasshopper poster, as a matter of fact—and just the moonlight on Ely Crescent started him off. He suddenly found himself thinking of a painter called Delvaux who did a lot of pictures of naked girls in moonlit landscapes. Under Charlotte's black coat there was a Delvaux girl, smooth and white, but he could not

17

tell her that. What he said was, 'I'd like to be up there among the stars. Flying like those clouds.'

She said nothing.

'It's all there if you want to see. All you have to do is look.'

Still she made no response, and when they came to a gap in the housefronts where a narrow road ran through to the market place, she turned into it. They were in shadow and he stepped in front of her and put his arms around her. She tilted her face away and kept her gloved hands close under her chin.

'What's wrong?'

'You are,' she said.

'Just because I insulted him? You don't have to worry, he had plenty of old women bleating around him.'

'It's not that.' She was so utterly motionless he could have had his arms around some fixed, padded object.

'What is it, then?' He moved one hand to touch her ear, but she drew away.

It was then that the grasshopper asserted itself, annoyingly. 'You had something to tell that man at the museum,' she accused him, 'but you wouldn't, not even when I asked you.'

'Because it was nonsense, that's why. A bloody song and dance about nothing.'

'It took you by surprise, anyway, so don't pretend it didn't. You've never seen a photograph of that grasshopper or whatever it is. You didn't think it really existed, did you?'

'Didn't care either.'

'Oh clever Harry Green! It's all beneath his dignity. He only shows me a poster of it that some old idiot gave him and tells me what a marvellous discovery it is, but when somebody shows him the real thing his poor little nose is put right out of joint and he don't want to know no more, do he?'

18

'He doesn't want to know any more because it is too stupid for words.' He let his voice assume an almost Beamish kind of drawl, correcting her, intending to anger her.

'It don't matter how stupid it is! You wouldn't even tell him where it came from.'

'I didn't have to, not with you around, gushing all over him.'

'Let me go.'

'And I don't *want* him to know where I got it.' He held her tighter as she tried to push away from him. 'I don't want him rootling around old Josh's place. He'd only get his dainty hands dirty.'

'What about your own dainty hands, Harry Green? I'm sure your mother wouldn't like where you've been with dirty old Josh Lovegrove—not her little boy.' She tried again to twist free but he crushed her. 'You're hurting!'

He shut his eyes. Now she was saying what every girl was supposed to say—'You're hurting!' What about him? The narrow street was carved in black and silver-grey, and across the gap in the rooftops above them the bright messages were flowing past. She would laugh if he told her what old Josh Lovegrove's place was really like.

'You should see your face!' she said. 'You look like a murderer.'

Her own face was painted by the moon in stabs of black shadow; eyes, nostrils and mouth. Harry saw a midnight flower, infinitely distant. He released her and stood back.

'You're right,' he said, 'it's a good night for a murder. I'd better walk home with you.'

'No.' Now she was getting her own back. Being cruel to him. 'I don't want you anywhere near me!'

She turned and ran. He made only a pretence of fol-

19

lowing her, but he watched until she had vanished into the shadows of the market square.

'Sod it!' He kicked the ground. All because of an idiotic imitation grasshopper. 'Sod it!'

3 Charlotte's Faults

It's surprising what you can hear if you're a good listener, which I am. People tell you things if you stay quiet and don't interrupt. It's just as if you're a kind of diary and they're putting things in it so they themselves can understand what they've been up to. It happens a lot. It happened with me and Charlotte so I know what she did that night after the lecture.

She had more pressing problems than grasshoppers on her mind, and as soon as she was out of Harry's sight she let the toes of her shoes drag along the frozen pavement. She wondered if she was being childish. But maybe Harry would find it cute and attractive. It didn't matter. She pulled her toes along the ground, sagging as she walked. It was as though she had ridden a pendulum to the bottom of its swing and had become heavy with its weight. She left the market place, heading towards the river.

Other girls wanted Harry Green. Several. The wind bit at her cheeks and she lowered her head.

It wasn't his looks—oh yes it was. What if his face did look as though it bruised too easily? At least he pushed it forward to *be* bruised.

She lifted her own head. The whole town had frozen and become metal and she was separated from it only by the thickness of her shoe sole. Harry Green. She didn't mind if he was a loser, but he didn't seem to realize that.

20

She loved him when he was battered. It was when he was a winner that he sulked, just as if he thought he didn't deserve it—as though winning belonged to other people.

'I never know where I am with you!' The words were in her mouth and out before she could stop them. She looked around quickly, afraid she had been overheard, but on such a night she was alone. Her own faults crowded in.

'My legs are too thick,' she said. 'My bottom's too big.'

She crossed the bridge and turned to go downstream. The river to her right was still in sight, but soon she would follow the bend of the road away from the river and go out towards Fairfield Drove.

'It's true!' But she knew it did not matter. To speak her faults under the moon was a charm to keep the rest of her looking as she did. Too pretty for Harry Green. Pretty enough for anybody. She must blot that out of her mind. 'My bum's too big!'

But she could say that only because she knew she was beautiful. People said so. Even girls said so. She began to run.

She ran with her toes pointing inwards and her heels kicking out sideways. She knew it was girlish. She knew boys liked it. She ran to where the Drove broadened before dividing into rows of small houses. The village of Fairfield was a further mile up the road, its church spire as thin and upright as a clock's hands at midnight.

She opened the wooden gate in the low railings of the front garden that was only big enough to take a bicycle, and unlocked the front door. Her mother was in the back room, laughing and surrounded by laughter from one of her funny shows, and the flickering telly light danced in her face.

'Did you remember to lock the door, Lottie?'

21

'It locks itself, don't it?'

'Because I don't want to be burglarized. They'll burglarize a person even at my age, them thugs.'

'You mean rape, don't you, Mother?'

'That an' all. Who'd you come home with? That young feller?' Then the screen triggered her and she laughed. 'He makes me die, that one. Look what he's doing with that girl.'

'What young feller is that?' But Charlotte knew her mother's interest in Harry; in anybody from that part of town.

'That boy you was telling me about. Him from Elizabeth Avenue. Him.' Then her temper sparked. 'Don't put the light on, I can't see properly.'

'That's over I should think, him and me.'

'I ain't surprised. Elizabeth Avenue.' And then, peevishly, 'What you want to put the light on for?'

'I'm looking for my books. I'm going upstairs.'

'You didn't come home on your own, did you? You know what Weldelph's like of a night-time.' Then the laughter accelerated, meshing like cogs and opening her mother's mouth to join in. 'Give us a kiss if you're on your way. Oh the cheeky sod, look what he's up to now!'

Her mother rarely asked for a kiss. She wanted to be alone with her programme. Charlotte switched the light off, and her mother's small face changed from old to ancient, hollowed out by the uncertain glow of the screen. She went over to peck at her mother's cheek and said, 'Where's Derek? Out?'

Her brother was forty.

'He had to do the thingummy, you know.' Derek had twice been to prison. Now he was having to do community service, but his mother never knew what to call it. 'I'd have made him fetch you if I'd known. It ain't safe nowadays for a girl on the streets.'

'Never was, Mum.'

'Look at where he's put his hand. That's what I call all-but. Was you going to do your homework?'

'I might.'

'I'll tell you one thing for nothin', them two don't have to go much further. He's all over her. It'll be the whole thing before long. On telly. Derek'll be a bit late, he said.'

The coldness of the night seemed to reach in and touch Charlotte's stomach. It was a burglar's moon out there. 'Did he say how late?'

'Do he ever? But it's that bitter I don't suppose they'll keep him long. What jobs have they got him on now?'

'He tidies old people's gardens.'

'At night?'

'No, Mother.'

'Well, I wish he'd tidy ours, if that's what he's doing. I can't stand this bit. Singin'. I don't think his singin'll get him anywhere, he just look as if he wants to roar, soppy-lookin' bugger.'

'He's better when he's just being mucky-minded.'

'That's what I say, Lottie. He's never a singer, not in a million years. It's just like Derek, he should never have got married. Sharon, she didn't give him no leeway. Even when he went out for a drink she wouldn't go with him.'

'Not with two little kids, I don't suppose she did.'

'That's what I mean. Stuck at home all the time. Never no social life; what sort of marriage is that? You can turn the sound up when you like; he can't go on much longer.'

'Sharon got custody anyway.'

'Cunning little bitch she is. Just what she always wanted—them kids all to herself, never mind about their father.'

Charlotte stood in a dim corner and looked at her illuminated mother. 'Goo' nigh', Mum,' she said.

'Nigh', Lottie. Sleep tight.'

23

Charlotte hung her coat on the back of the kitchen door and went quickly out into the yard and into the lavatory. Derek's cigarette smoke lingered there. The seat was icy so she poised herself just clear of it. There was no light. Little triangles of night sky showed at the top of the door.

Out there, a mile away in the churchyard under the spire, her father lay. All she remembered was an old man. A grey face, and eyes that sagged with redness. He had been under the frozen grass ever since she was three. She shivered.

What was it that Harry Green knew about grass-hoppers and wouldn't say? He did know something else, you could tell. And that museum man had been offended. But not by her. She allowed herself, suddenly warm, to think of Hugh Beamish's dark face and the way he had looked at her. She shivered again before she stood up.

4 Just a Minuet

My father knows Mrs Frost, who is a part-time assistant at Weldelph Museum, and she told him what happened the morning after the lecture. In a funny kind of way it had something to do with the grasshopper, but nobody realized it at the time, and it also explained why Harry had said 'pict-you-are' in that strange way and offended Hugh Beamish.

The museum hadn't long been opened that morning when a small man came in and began scrubbing his feet so hard on the doormat that he seemed determined to do a Rumpelstiltskin and go right through the floor. The sound brought Hugh Beamish into the foyer and he didn't like what he saw. The little man, he thought, must be one of those shambling wanderers drawn to the museum to stand by a radiator and exude fumes until Mrs Frost stumped in and swept them out like autumn leaves to find a warm cranny somewhere else.

I quite like Hugh, in spite of what he did later, and he certainly had a lot to put up with from Mrs Frost. She was ferocious and she could just as easily turn against him as against anyone else—'This is a museum, Mr Beamish, not a doss house'—because she considered he was weak-willed and didn't do enough to repel visitors. Well I suppose he was weak-willed, or he'd still be here, but that morning he'd come into the foyer determined to do something about the small man with the red and white woollen cap and the oversize overcoat that hung to his ankles.

'Can I,' said Hugh, 'do anything to help you?' He spoke with such appalling politeness that even a bishop would have been quelled. The little man's head jerked up and he smiled but said nothing.

'Good morning to you.' Hugh threw a new slab of greeting towards the silver stubble of the small face. 'In what way can we assist you?'

A voice from under the cap responded. 'It's a pleshuar,' it said.

There was a pause for Hugh's disdain to rear itself. 'A what?' he said.

'A pleshuar to meet you, Mr Beamuish. A very great pleshuar indeed.'

'Oh really?' said Hugh, and it was then that an echo stirred in his mind.

'I read about you in the papuar,' said the man.

Hugh spoke with caution. 'The local paper—is that what you mean?'

The small, round head nodded vigorously. 'I recognized you from your pict-you-are.'

'Ah!' Recognition struck. Hugh remembered Harry and at the same time realized that nobody had been taking the mickey out of him the night before. We had all been laughing at the wah-wah accent of the little man. And, give Hugh his due, he played up to it right from the start.

'Yes, of course,' he said to the tramp, because that's what he took the little man to be—wrong, but that's the way it was—'you must have seen my pictuar in the papuar.'

'You,' said the small face, looking up from so many coils of grey scarf it was like a cobra rising from its basket, 'are a spiduar.' The footscrubbing ceased. 'An intellectual spiduar at the centre of your web. There will not be much in the whole of Weldelph and the lands beyond that escapes your attention, Mr Beamuish.'

Hugh wondered if, like a spider, he should scuttle back into his office and digest the new name he had been given. He was beginning to have doubts about the way he should react. The little man sounded like a social climber whose accent-hunting had gone way over the top, yet his clothes said something different. He didn't give Hugh a chance to make up his mind.

'Allow me to put you to the test, Mr Beamuish.'

He had a walking stick which he hung over his arm before he stepped from the doormat. The squeal that the thick crepe soles of his shoes made on the lino halted him. He paused and then advanced more carefully with a rocking motion like a man wearing a pair of desk blotters on his feet. Hugh noticed that his trousers were tucked into his socks, probably to prevent the cold air outside going up his legs. As he crossed the foyer, swaying like a pendulum, he unhooked the stick from his arm and held it out. 'Tell me, if you are able, what this is.'

Hugh took the stick. It was thin and pale and brownly mottled, narrowing almost to a point at its tip. 'A cane?' he said.

'No,' said the little man.

26

Hugh twisted the handle and found no join. 'Not a swordstick,' he mused.

'No steel. No blade. Nothing is hidden,' said the man.

'But covered in a sort of parchment.' Hugh examined it closer. He flourished it, humouring the little man who grinned through his stubble. 'Not a swordstick, but sharp enough to give a good prod.'

The grin did not lessen.

'The tusk of a narwhal?'

A shake of the head.

'The horn of a unicorn? A stick of barleysugar? A gardening implement for planting beans?'

The head shook and a mittened hand came forward to take the stick. 'May I trouble you for my bull's pizzle, young man?'

Hugh had heard of such things but had never before seen one. He looked down at the elegant cane and noticed that he was now holding it by his fingertips. 'How curious,' he said, and released it into the mittens.

Unexpectedly, the voice from the stubble apologized. 'I do beg your pardon.'

'Not at all.' Hugh was rubbing his palms against his trouser legs, but it was not triumph over the bull's relic that brought the sudden apology. The little man was embarrassed at stepping into Hugh's domain without removing his headgear. He snatched the red and white stripes from his head.

'My football hat,' he said, rather shamefaced. 'It's an indulgence of mine.'

'Rugguar?' said Hugh, pressing home his advantage.

'Rugguar rubbuish!' The blue eyes were as sharp as a chipped plate. 'Soccuar's the only game around here.'

Hugh swayed slightly. No words came.

'Well, young felluar, I have told you about pizzles, so what can you tell me about rope?'

'Rope?'

27

'Rope through the ages ...' becoming businesslike '... twines, strings, cordages. I would like to know about a certain rope-like substuance. A gut.'

Mrs Frost had heard it all. Her typewriter had ceased stuttering from the moment the conversation began, and now she knew her help was needed. Even before Hugh had had a chance to summon her she had opened the office door and was pounding across the floor towards him.

'You have a problem, Mr Beamish?' She ignored the visitor.

'Yes, Mrs Frost. Rope. What have we on rope?' I can imagine how forlornly he gazed into her broad but compressed face. 'Or gut,' he added, smiling sweetly.

'Nothing on gut.' Mrs Frost's face was squeezed into horizontal folds, from one of which she spoke. 'Rope? Did you say rope, Mr Beamish?'

She saw Hugh smile and lean towards her submissively. It seemed to her that he only just resisted the urge to put his hands in his sleeves, squint his eyes and grovel like a slave of the lamp. 'This gentleman has expressed a desire to know about rope, Mrs Frost.' His head remained bowed, as though awaiting the executioner's axe.

Mrs Frost always spoke as if she was reading a label. 'Gallery three,' she said. 'Case B, middle shelf. Model of a ropewalk.'

'A model. Of course. Marvellous. I do hope that helps you, sir.'

'There's nothing else.' Mrs Frost turned about and thudded away. 'No gut.'

If Hugh Beamish had only realized it, he was at that moment very close to the secret of the grasshopper. Gut was the clue, but he could hardly have been expected to know it. Mrs Frost had reached the alcove leading to the office and she turned to see that he had bent so far forward that his face was now level with the little man's

28

unshaven chin, and she heard him say, almost with a servile whine, 'Will there be anything else?'

'You have your work to do, Mr Beamuish,' said the man. 'I shall disturb you no longuar.' He turned and commenced an elaborate tiptoe. 'I shall be as silent as if these shoes were slippuars.'

Hugh was aware of a slightly theatrical stagger as he entered his office behind Mrs Frost and shut the door. 'Who,' he asked, 'was *that*?'

She was turning over papers on his desk. 'Old Lovegrove,' she said. 'He's not short of a quid.'

'He looks poverty-strickuen.'

'Strick what?' She turned her head sharply.

'He looks poor.'

'Him? Old Josh?'

'Josh? Did you say Josh?' Hugh's eyes glazed. 'He can't really be called Josh-you-are, can he?'

'Yes, he is. And worth a mint, so they say.'

'So it's not Joshua the paupuar.' He sat down, slumped over his desk, and Mrs Frost recoiled to see his shoulders shake. She thought he was weeping.

'Are you all right, Mr Beamish?' she asked.

'I shall be fine in a minuet, Mrs Frost,' he said. 'I am just temporarily bugguared.'

5 Joshua's Quest

I'll admit I am sometimes writing a bit more than I actually saw or heard, but nobody knows as much as I do about what happened, and if you don't let your imagination reach out you'll never learn the full truth about anything. That grasshopper, for instance. I knew from the moment it popped up on that screen that there was more to it than anybody, even Charlotte, seemed to realize. My imagination just gave a click, like a very small door opening somewhere inside, and when I looked through it I knew I just had to go on. Which is why, next morning, I found myself in the Paradise Café. I'd followed Harry Green there.

The sun in winter rarely reaches far into the frozen cleft of Scrapeshin's Passage, and never as far as the glass door of the Paradise. The windows were steamed up, an urn hissed behind the counter, the cardboard boxes which had been flattened out to protect the floor tiles were grey with footprints, and cigarette smoke lay in the air like the marbling on the edges of an old book.

I was there illegally, and so was Harry, but we sat at separate tables partly because we still didn't know each other and partly because he was talking to somebody else. Harry had quite a glamorous way of getting out of school at breaktime—through the bog window and out on to the quay—and I had done the same thing without him knowing anything about it. He was a bit touchy about other people copying his heroics. And I also wasn't surprised to see him head for the Paradise because Harry wanted everybody to think of him as a low-lifer, and the Paradise suited his image.

What I intended to get from following him was so vague it hardly existed, so what actually happened was a bonus—although it was no surprise to see him talking to Joshua Lovegrove because old Josh was everybody's favourite in the sixth. There was a lot of Josh-you-are-speak in the common room, and everybody knew of the bull's whatnot. Most people made fun of old Josh, but Harry was taking him seriously. He didn't even see me come in and stand at the counter. He was watching Josh pick open the wrapper of a chocolate wafer and nibble it like a squirrel with an acorn.

Harry kept his voice down, but I heard him say, 'It was practically the same as that poster you showed me.'

There was that click in my head. My mind saw the

grasshopper picture, and my timing was perfect. I sat down quietly at the table behind Harry's back, just as Josh answered him.

'Hardly large enough to be called a postuar,' he said. 'I term it a handbill.'

'Handbill, then.' I could see that the feverish, chiselling precision of the little man was irritating Harry. 'But it was a real photograph, Josh, and it was exactly the same as the handbill.'

'My uncle threw nothing away,' said Josh. 'I have the same pictuar.'

I wanted to know about Josh's uncle, but Harry seemed to have other things on his mind. He pushed himself back in his seat and looked away. The smoke hung heaviest over the corner table where the dockers from the quay murmured with their backs to the room. One of them wore a black donkey jacket with the name of his firm stencilled across the shoulders, MATES. The white letters were louder than their voices, and Harry seemed to feel it would be unwise to disturb them. He put his elbows on the table and said quietly, 'I suppose your uncle is the man in the photograph.'

'As a matter of fact my great-uncle. Great-uncle Cox and his Animals; I was under the impression that I had told you that, young sir.'

'You didn't say it was your uncle,' said Harry, then corrected himself, 'great-uncle, I mean.'

'He had mustachios like the horns of a water buffalo.'

'I've seen his photograph. You didn't tell me about that either.'

The little man sat with his woollen cap in his lap, nibbled and said nothing. His scalp showed through the white bristles of his close-cropped hair and he could have been a bantam-weight boxer or my idea of a French playwright just out of jail with the shadow of the guillotine lingering in the pink folds of his neck. He was mild, but he was no joke.

31

'What else have you got?' Harry asked.

'I have the pizzle of a bull.' The cane rested against his knees. 'What else do I need?' He rapped it on the floor, and the MATES man glanced over his shoulder. 'Sorry to disturb you,' said Josh. 'I was just demonstrating something to this young fellnar.'

Everybody knew Josh. The man said, 'Don't worry about it, old cock,' and turned away. But the fact that they had been overheard made Harry lower his voice even further. 'Nobody in the museum knew what the grasshopper was, Mr Lovegrove,' he said. I leant forward at this and I could just see Harry glance apprehensively towards the dockers. There wasn't much heroism in him just then. He was afraid of them, and it showed. Old Josh had become Mr Lovegrove because he wanted the dockers to see that he was being nice to the old man. But he had to know more about the grasshopper. 'The people last night thought it was some sort of ride at the Mart,' he said, 'something off a roundabout. Was it? Do *you* know what it was?'

Josh munched.

Harry said, 'I won't tell anyone anything if you don't want me to.'

It was about to get interesting, but they were interrupted. The café door swung suddenly inwards and the dangling Open sign clattered against the glass. Trigger Harris, as always, came in with a bang. 'Ha!' He spotted Harry and pointed his rat face and rimless glasses in his direction. 'I find you drinking rum with a sailor in a slum!'

The MATES shoulders began to turn, and Harry winced. So did I. There's something about Trigger that makes you want to be somewhere else most of the time. He was older than us, but still hanging around the Upper Sixth in search of some obscure qualification or other, and he was an embarrassment, definitely. Harry, for some reason which I wasn't aware of then, seemed to be a favourite of his. Poor Harry.

'I find you drinking beer with a Bavarian,' said Trigger, louder. Even worse, it was a poem. 'I find you drinking gin in the lowest kind of inn, because you are a rigid vegetarian!'

'Shut that bloody door!' said the MATES man.

'Sit down, Trigger.' Harry got to his feet. 'I'll fetch you a coffee.'

'Uncommon decent of you, Harry lad.' Trigger bent a knee to take off his cycle clips, and began unwinding the thin scarf that, tucked into his jacket, was his only protection against the cold. 'Nice to see you, Joshua.'

'And you, too, young Trigguar.'

Trigger grinned and hissed in and out between his teeth, his version of laughter. 'Not so young as some, Mr Lovegrove.'

'Nor so old as others.'

'You are good for my self-esteem.' Trigger twisted in his seat to look towards Harry at the counter. 'Our young friend takes his life in his hands to come here, you know, Josh. It is an illicit use of breaktime.'

'Jewels,' said Joshua Lovegrove. He finished eating his biscuit and looked up. 'No matter where you care to look there are jewels.'

Trigger lifted his eyes towards a calendar showing a beach girl with breasts brushed as smooth as amber sand dunes. 'It depends upon one's tastes, of course, but I do agree that the art work, even in a greasy spoon joint such as this, is quite exceptional.'

'Jewels.' Josh held out a mitten in which the shiny wrapper of his biscuit glinted in many colours.

Harry returned with the coffee, and Trigger looked up at him. 'Mr Lovegrove is showing me a fistful of treasure,' he said, 'and all for twenty p.'

'Less costly even than that,' said Josh, 'and just look at the shine.'

'Wonderful!' Trigger turned his grin on Harry. 'Such exquisite workmanship should be preserved for eternity.'

The wrapper was being smoothed on the table. Now Josh tapped it with a fingernail. 'If this had just been discovered in an Egyptian tomb I would not be allowed to touch it. Under glass. Too precious. Did you ever see silver with a shine like that? There never was an ancient blue as deep as that blue. And that red—you could dip your fingers into that red.' The round stubble of the face came up. 'Where did you ever see anything as pretty as that?'

'Everywhere,' said Harry, very cleverly I thought.

'Stap me,' said Trigger, 'a couple of philosophers.'

Josh ignored him. He was keeping his eyes on Harry. 'And gut?' he asked. 'What do you know about gut?'

'I can tell by the blankness of that handsome face,' said Trigger, 'that he knows precious little about gut.' He was laughing, sucking in and out. 'Gut? Why gut? And why ask Harry? All he knows about is young ladies, alas.'

'Not any more,' said Harry.

'Not even the divine Charlotte?' Trigger's eyes gleamed behind his glasses. It was a greedy look and I was glad it wasn't directed my way. 'There is a rift?' he asked. All Harry did was shrug, but Trigger took it as agreement. 'I'm delighted to hear it. Charlotte up for grabs again—that is, if one's tastes should run in that particular direction.'

Harry looked to Josh to rescue him. 'I don't know anything about gut,' he said.

'You are not the first this morning,' said Josh. 'I have already put the question to young Mr Beamuish.'

Harry remembered the name. 'You've been to the museum?' he asked.

34

'Beamuish is at the nub of learning but he was quite unable to assist. My quest for gut continues.'

Beamish. The museum. The grasshopper. And Josh. Idiotic connections, leaping like clowns, bounded into my mind and linked arms. Harry seemed to be on to it as well. 'Gut,' he said suddenly. 'Why gut? What is gut anyway? I don't know anything about gut.'

Josh bowed his head and was reaching within the coils of his scarf. 'On the contrary, young felluar, you may know everything about gut.' He placed something on the table. 'I do not doubt that you have seen one of these before.'

I couldn't help leaning forward, but Trigger was the only one to see the movement. I doubt whether he recognized me but he winked and tilted the object, without the others being aware of what he was doing, so that I could see what it was. It was a booklet, no more than about eight pages, but I could see Harry's name— Harold Green—printed in a very florid lettering across the front.

Trigger even read aloud what he saw. 'Harold Green and Son, Seedsmen and Agricultural Suppliers.' He turned the first page. 'Harry's family firm,' he said. 'Looks like a price list.'

'The first one,' said Harry. 'My father's got one in the warehouse. But it's very tatty.' This was hardly surprising as it was more than a century old.

'Seed potatoes,' said Trigger, still reading. 'Chitting trays, chip baskets.' He turned the pages. 'This is how the family fortune was founded, Harry, scythes and sack barrows.'

'Turn,' said the little man, 'to the last page.' Trigger did so. 'And what do you see under Farm Tackle?'

'Binder twine. Chains. Straps. Rope.'

'Harry Green,' said Josh, interrupting, 'is there any old stock remaining in your warehouse?'

'There might be. I don't know.' The glittering eyes held him. 'Why?'

'Near the bottom of the page.' Josh spoke to Trigger. 'What see you there?'

'Ha!' Trigger's shout of laughter stirred the MATES shoulders. 'Guts, various. Don't we all need some?'

A grunt from the MATES corner sounded very much like 'piss off', but Josh seemed not to hear. He took the price list from Trigger and handed it to Harry. 'My compliments to your fathuar,' he said, 'and would he oblige me by searching his warehouse?'

'What for?' said Harry.

'Gut,' said Josh. 'American Gut.'

PART TWO

6 A Hook in the Nook

I am in an embarrassing position. My father is a teacher at Weldelph Comp, the same school as me, which means that I'm caught in the middle, between them and us, or what he in his witty way refers to as the gamekeepers and the poachers. But we've got a system—when there's anybody within earshot he calls me by my surname, Williams, and I have been known to call him sir. We always manage to do it straightfaced, so it's acting of a very high order.

I've got to admit that having your old man in the academic racket has some hidden plus points, even if you aren't aware of them at the time. I mean, all you have to do is show a squeak of interest in something and the next thing you know he's dumping a book in front of you or dragging you off somewhere in the pursuit of learning, such as a museum. But it goes much further than that.

When one day I breathed a hint of enthusiasm for writing I was whisked round to the office of the Weldelph *Messenger* and we met the editor and everybody. *Very* embarrassing, except for one thing. We met Robin Horn. I liked him right from the kick-off, and so did Dad; in fact he and Robin became boozing partners, or so my mother says. She reckons that what stops Dad becoming a headmaster, or even head of his department, is that somebody has written on his secret dossier: 'Likes a pint.' Well, so does Robin Horn, chief reporter—or that's what he was until the scandal broke.

My father, little did he know it, was in the pub when it all began.

It was only a couple of days after our trip to the *Messenger* office so when Robin came into the bar with another guy my father didn't push himself forward, although he recognized the other man and he later got to know him nearly as well as I did. It was Hugh Beamish from the museum, and the grasshopper was already treading on his heels.

It was Robin's technique for making life easy that amused my father. Robin's face, Dad said, was too smooth and round for thirty. He looked like a child who had stolen his father's cigarettes and was wearing a false moustache, which was so fair it hardly showed. And he was in full song as he came through the door with Hugh Beamish. 'Sorry I couldn't get to your talk last night, old boy,' he said. 'Office diary to blame. Pages stuck together.'

'Not to worry,' said Hugh Beamish. 'No harm done.'

Robin nodded towards my father, then turned back to Hugh. 'Not a bad watering hole once they get to know you, old boy.' Then he spoke to the man with the ruby-red face and tight collar behind the bar. 'George,' he said, 'this is our new master of the revels at the museum.' Just the sort of phrase to keep my father happy.

'Pleased to meet you, sir.' A head of hair like two smooth grey tiles, one each side of the parting, was tilted in Hugh's direction.

'Give the gentleman his pleasure, George.'

'Bitter,' said Hugh. 'Pump not keg.'

'And a thimbleful for me, George.'

'Glass or tankard, sir?' the barman asked Hugh.

'Tankard, please.'

A fist like a bunch of soft carrots mated with a china pump handle and pulled two pints. Hugh later admitted he made a mistake in believing that the large reporter in the check suit was a tankard man. Robin's beer came in a glass without a handle, even though tankards seemed more appropriate to the bar itself. It is a tiny room with a sloping ceiling because it is squeezed under the hotel's main staircase. The bar counter makes an oak curve in the corner, and there is room for only three circular tables. Very much a tankard place.

Robin Horn's moustache pricked the foam of his pint. 'Welcome to the nook and cranny, old boy.' He eyed Hugh's tankard. 'You likee?'

'Pretty fair.' Hugh sipped and then said the right thing. 'Temperature spot on. Not iced, and not warm either.'

'Cradled in a maiden's bra,' said Robin. 'He likes your cellar-work, George, have a gargle yourself.'

'Thank you, Mr Horn. I'll take a cordial.' A tiny shot glass filled with a colourless spirit was tossed into a hole under the tiles.

'George is a repository,' said Robin.

'I can believe it.' Hugh raised his tankard to the barman.

'Not a booze repository, old boy. A mine of information. George, is young Mr Beamish worth a hook?'

'I should think so, Mr Horn. He appears to know his ale.'

The reporter's round face beamed on him. 'Drink up, old boy. You've just been allocated a hook in the nook.'

'A what?'

'A place to hang your tankard. You're *in*, old son.'

'How gratifying.' Hugh's voice had an academic whinny which, my father reckons, he tried to cover up. 'Will you have a cordial on me, George?'

'I'll bide my time, sir.' But he reached for the tankard and Robin's glass, which was already empty.

Apart from my father, there were as yet no other customers in the nook, and Hugh followed Robin to a seat in the corner. 'It's very cosy in here,' he said. 'Cosier than my office.'

'Or the reporters' room. Good of you to come in, old boy. After me missing your lecture.'

'It was excessively dull.'

'Not what I heard. Old Pukey told me you were wonderful.' Robin raised his voice. 'Hey, George, has the Puke changed his underpants yet?'

'Not to my knowledge, Mr Horn.'

'Nor mine, thank God.' Robin turned back to Hugh. 'You're not a source close to Pukey Puckeridge's under-wear, are you?'

My father had been as puzzled as Hugh Beamish, but at that moment enlightenment dawned. Alfred Puck-eridge was editor of the *Messenger*.

'Little sod gave me a right rollicking over missing your talk,' said Robin. 'You didn't shake him by the hand did you?'

'I believe I did.'

'Never mind, old son, you can always get a skin graft. Another brew?'

Hugh's pot was still a quarter full, but Robin took the tankard to the bar and returned with it brimming. 'Old George gave you a long pull, Mr Beamish.'

'Hugh,' said Hugh.

'Robin,' said Robin.

A pause ensued. Even though there were still only three customers, the little room looked occupied. Robin's sheepskin coat lay over a stool near the bar, and his cigarettes and his lighter lay on the counter next to where he had left his change. He was searching his pock-ets. 'You don't have a bit of paper do you, Hugh? I've come without my notebook.'

'That's very remiss of a reportuar.'

'A what-you-are, old boy?'

'A reportuar. And I was told you were the *chief* reportuar.'

My father was pleased with himself because, even though we'd been in Weldelph for only a few months, he picked up the reference to Joshua Lovegrove just as quickly as the reporter. He had no idea that the grasshopper was taking a step nearer.

'Gotcha!' Robin had found a ballpoint. 'So old Joshua has nobbled you already.'

'He wanted to know about rope.'

'Josh isn't into bondage, is he? Paper, Hugh?'

Hugh reached to his inside pocket. 'I happen to have the text of last night's lecture,' he said.

Robin unfolded the sheets. 'And typed! Old boy, you've saved my life. I was going to have to take notes, but now I don't.' He bunched the papers and put them in his breast pocket. 'Office closed. Time to reward honest labour. Your jar, Hugh.' He waited until Hugh had drained the tankard. 'You're not married, are you? You don't have to dash home to squeeze a lemon or anything?'

'Not married, no, and nothing like that, not yet. But last night . . .' He checked himself; the beer was beginning to talk.

'You've been talent-spotting already,' said Robin. 'Naughty.'

'More naughty than you think. She's very good-looking. Exceptionally. But quite out of reach.'

'We're talking about the museum chairman's wife, are we?'

'Mrs Lockyer wasn't there last night,' said Hugh, 'so it wasn't the chairman's wife I was talking about. Someone even better-looking.'

'She takes a bit of beating does the divine Lockyer. I wouldn't mind being in your position, Hugh, close to that beautiful bosom.'

'If I ever stray in that direction I'll let you know.'

41

'Don't bother,' said the reporter.

'I should've thought you'd have gone in for a bit of shock-horror, Robin.'

'So I would, old son. But the *Messenger* is the Puke's baby—and he offends no one.'

'Unless you're a source close to his underwear.'

'You're catching on, Hugh.' Robin drank. 'This beer hasn't gone off, has it?'

'I don't think we've given it time.'

'Better have a quickie in case it does.'

My father was very amused.

7 'Write me lovely'

'The trouble with you,' said Charlotte, 'is that you act as though you are in a book.'

'Maybe I am,' said Harry.

'Maybe you are. I wouldn't be surprised. You can afford to be.'

'Afford to be? There's no afford about it. I'm in this sixth form common room, aren't I?' Harry looked around him. They were in the old part of the building, a former classroom that, with the library, was joined to the headmaster's house. 'Windows like a church and just as bloody draughty. *I* can afford to be here, *you* can afford to be here. If I'm in a story, *you* are in a story.'

'Not the same one.'

'If we are in the same place at the same time it *has* to be the same one.'

'It was the same one until you got so bloody nasty last night,' she said.

'Swearing,' he said, 'doesn't suit you.'

'But *you* can swear, that's all right. You can swear because it's what men do. Well, I can swear because it's

42

the way people speak who live where I do. And don't try to tell me you don't know that.' She spoke quickly, knowing he wanted to interrupt. 'As a matter of fact I said bloody because I needed a bloody adjective, and you *were* nasty last night, bloody nasty. So if you still want to dominate and be class-conscious like the little rich boy you are—buy me a coffee.'

'Buy your own,' said a skinny, long-haired youth who had been standing nearby.

'Who asked you to poke your nose in?' said Harry. 'I'll buy her a coffee only if I want to.' The pale youth shrugged and wandered away. 'Who is he, anyway? What right has he to tell anybody to do anything?'

'Maybe he's the one who's telling the story,' said Charlotte. 'The one you're in. If he's writing it, you want to keep in his good books.' She laughed, but Harry made no response. 'And if it was me who was writing the story,' she said, 'I would put in just what I was thinking, like Virginia Woolf.'

'Sex,' he said, 'that's all it is with her.'

'She's good at that, I admit. But she also tells you what people think and that's the most important thing of all. Wouldn't you like to know what I'm thinking, *all* my thoughts, *all* the time?'

'All I can ever know is what I'm thinking,' he said. 'I don't know your thoughts.'

'So you'd better start reading the story, then maybe you would know. Every story needs a reader or it doesn't make sense.'

'You don't make sense to me.'

'Oh, Harry, don't be so dumb. Why can't you pretend we're in the same story and that somebody is reading us—all about how desirable I am, and what a squashed-up face you've got. All that. He's with us now, the reader.' She shivered, delighted at the game they could play. If he would. 'It's a very funny thing being in a story—once you know you're in it.' She looked up at

43

the ceiling as though it was a page. 'Reader,' she said, 'love me.'

He sat stolidly in his chair. She embarrassed him, wanting to share thoughts, in public. 'I don't mind reading you,' he said, 'but I don't want to have to write you as well.'

'But that's just what you've got to do, Harry. Write me, darling. Write me lovely.' She leant forward, playing the actress, but only half her intensity was play-acting. She really did want him to invent her, so that she could invent him in return and then they would truly be in the same story, writing and reading together. She was prepared to lose herself, to him. He saw it, and backed away. He could not reveal himself so easily.

'What sort of scene are we in now?' he asked, pretending to play her game but running from her as fast as he could. 'Are we tragic or comic?'

She had been leaning forward. Now she straightened. 'Charlotte's herself again,' she said. Her blush had turned to paleness. 'I can't afford to be in your story, Harry, because you're better off than me, and when you leave this *common* room your life is different.'

He had a sudden glimpse of what he had done. She had offered him a kind of heaven and he had been afraid to enter. Now she was shutting the door on him. 'Charlotte,' he said.

She looked at him calmly but said nothing.

'Charlotte, it's a dull story that only thinks about things outside itself—like how much money people have got.'

'But money *does* affect them, Harry—the way they act. The way *you* act.'

'And you.'

'Yes, the lack of it. I have to think of things you don't know anything about. Like having an outside loo and wanting to go for a pee in the middle of the night.'

'A pot under the bed,' he said.

'And what do you know about that? Nothing.'

'You don't even have to open the bedroom door,' he said. 'Or go across the landing. You pee in the dark and it's nice and warm. Very cosy.'

'Now you're sneering.'

'No, I'm not. I don't care what you pee in.'

'Thank you very much.'

Laughter might have worked. The barrier would have broken if either had caught the other's eye. But neither dared do it.

'Anyway,' he said, looking at the grey floorboards between the worn edges of two old carpets, 'how do you mean I act as though I'm in a story?'

'I keep thinking about you and that grasshopper picture last night,' said Charlotte. 'I thought that picture was so strange I wanted to know more and more about it, like an adventure story. But you didn't care. You were just like you normally are. You acted as you always do—as if you know what's going to happen. It's just as if everything's already in place, laid out, and all you've got to do is carry on as you are. But me, I can't. If I let go I shall start sliding, faster and faster, and then I shall be falling and I shan't be able to stop.'

He knew she was right about both of them. But she was wrong about him having no worries on his mind. And even if his family was better off than hers, she didn't have to make so much of it.

'So I'm a cocky little rich kid,' he said. 'Is that it?'

'That's part of it. I know where you were at breaktime this morning—you were out at the Paradise caff, just having a dare like a kid in a story.'

'Some pretty tough characters get there,' he said. 'They don't care what story I'm supposed to be in. You have to watch your step.'

'But you can step straight out of it whenever you want to. If I went there it would be because it was the only place I could afford.'

'You'd better buy her a coffee after all.' The skinny youth, who had been listening all the time, had wandered back to where they were sitting.

'Look, mate,' Harry leant back in the springless armchair, 'I don't know if you're trying to be funny, but this is none of your bloody business.'

'Well said,' said the youth. 'I couldn't have put it better myself.'

'Sod off,' said Harry. For a moment he thought the youth was going to retaliate, and the old despicable jolt of anxiety made him panic. But the thin face smiled and turned away, and the youth wandered off.

'You've got a nasty temper, Harry Green.' Charlotte got to her feet. 'That boy was only having a bit of fun with you, but you were as bad as you were last night with Mr Beamish.'

'*Hugh* Beamish to you. He made sure of getting that in.'

'You're being stupid.'

'Well, why are you blushing?'

'Because you are making me furious!' She stood over him. 'All I wanted you to do was tell him about those fairground animals. That's all. But you were just like a sulky little kid who wanted to keep a secret!'

Harry looked up at her, trying to see unprettyness in her face to turn his mind against her. Her mouth was close to crying, and that made it easier.

'As a matter of fact,' he said, 'I should think I can get to know even more about those grasshoppers and things. I saw old Josh Lovegrove this morning and he wants me to do something for him.'

He paused long enough to make her say, 'Well, what is it he wants?'

She had put herself in his power. He leant back in the threadbare upholstery.

'Are you going to tell me?' Charlotte asked.

'I shouldn't think so.'

46

'Do you mean that?'

She had suddenly become serious. It could easily turn sour. It was up to him.

'Are you going to tell me?' she repeated.

'No.'

He watched her turn and leave. The dust of the armchair had a bitter smell. He allowed himself to enjoy it.

The skinny youth, who had watched all this, wandered closer and sat down, and that was how I got to know Harry.

8 King John's Lakes

I once stared at the wallpaper in my room for so long that I actually sank through the pattern, which was a garden trellis with rosebuds, and found myself walking in the landscape beyond it, going across the lawns and up to the house in the distance. It wasn't long after we'd moved here, as a matter of fact, and the wallpaper had been put up by somebody else, but I grew to like it, going for those walks, and it certainly told me a lot about the person who chose it. I also grew to like him— or her.

And the Weldelph Scandal is a bit like that. You have to stare at it before you get into it and come close to the grasshopper. I don't think Mrs Nina Lockyer ever did see it, even though she was as close to it as anybody. The trouble with her is that she doesn't notice anything unless it really touches her. Because she already has everything. She's old enough to be my mother but she's dark-haired and smooth and terrifically good-looking. She knows she is, so she smiles all the time in a gracious kind of way. She's also the biggest snob I've ever seen. And rich. Everybody in Weldelph calls her Lady Lockyer.

I was walking past her house on my way home when I looked up and saw her in the window. 'Darling,' she said. I know she said it because I saw her lips move in the darling way, and it took me straight through the window just as if it was wallpaper.

'Darling.' She was speaking to her husband, Mr Lacey Lockyer. 'I never saw such an immense bunch of keys in my life! What can he have locked away in that peculiar place of his?'

They were talking about Joshua Lovegrove and King John's Lakes, and some of this came out in the court case later. When she was in the witness box, Nina Lockyer went flat out to give a good impression, so she said far too much. Stupid things. She even told everybody what Lacey Lockyer said about Josh's bunch of keys— he doubted whether more than one in twenty had a lock to open, and he reminded her that old Josh lived among piles of junk.

'But he seemed such a clean old man,' she said, 'and it was a *lovely* bunch of keys. *So* in character.'

'I suppose you realize,' he told her, 'that King John's Lakes are no more than a rubbish tip. Rotting mattresses—the lot.'

'I can't believe it. He looked so sweet—and *bristly*.'

'Bristly?' said Lacey. 'Unshaven, you mean.'

'But such clean little silvery bristles.' She shuddered and looked out of the bow window in which they were sitting having lunch. Their house is one of the Georgian fronts that line the long curve of the river through the town. It's called The Sweep, and faces south to get the best of the sunshine. On the other bank of the river, but further upstream and well out of sight, is King John's Lakes.

'He was fishing into the depths of that absurd overcoat he wears,' she said, 'looking for something to show the museum people, and all those keys came out. He quite failed to find what he was looking for, and then I

48

came in and spoiled it. You know how ridiculously polite he becomes—at least he always does when I'm there, quite embarrassingly so, and nothing, but *nothing*, would induce him to continue.' She smiled across the table. 'Old Josh is *such* a character, darling. The town would not be the same without him.'

'I quite agree, darling. He ought to have a preservation order slapped on him.'

They both laughed. 'Or that nice young man at the museum could pop him into a glass case. I wonder I didn't think to ask him.'

'So you liked our Hugh Beamish, did you?' her husband asked.

'Charming. We must have him round for supper one evening. Yes, darling?'

'Yes, darling.'

The bow window was above pavement level and jutted out like a box in a theatre—except that Nina Lockyer seemed to think it was she who was on the stage with the railings and the basement area below the window forming the orchestra pit. That meant that the sun gathered by the great dish of The Sweep was focused directly onto the elegant set that she had made of the room. It also spotlighted the dialogue.

'They say old Josh is frightfully rich,' she said.

'On the analogy, I suppose, that every tramp must have a large bank balance.' Lacey was cutting an apple into segments. They had been having a light lunch, brought in on a tray. 'No, darling, old Josh-you-are may, in fact, be a miz-you-are, but he is also as poor as he looks, I can assure you.'

'He certainly cuts a strange fig-you-are.'

Nina Lockyer laughed. She doesn't look as though she's old enough to have a teenage daughter, or so my father says, and anyway nobody seems to have seen this girl because she's been sent away to school so that Weldelph won't have a chance to contaminate her accent. I could see the pearls that were warmed by Nina Lockyer's neck, and her green eyes were as wide as a cat's.

'But seriously, darling,' she said, 'if anyone knows what Mr Lovegrove is worth it must be you.'

From where she sat she could see his name in golden letters in his office window across the river. It said he was an 'enterprise consultant', but I've heard him called other things. My father says you can't turn over a stone in Weldelph without finding 'the consultant' lurking underneath, taking his cut.

'I don't handle the affairs of everybody in this town,' Lacey Lockyer told his wife, 'even though you flatter me by thinking so. Old Lovegrove's books, if he has any, are closed to me.'

'But there's the land,' she said. 'Mr Lovegrove is a landowner. Surely King John's Lakes are quite big.'

Her husband told her the Lakes were worthless and far too marshy for any useful purpose.

'But they must be oozing with history.' Her fingers fluttered in the sunshine. 'I would wager with you, Lacey my sweet, that King John's Treasure is supposed to be buried there.'

He laughed when she said that, and I don't blame him. King John is said to have lost the Crown Jewels of England when his baggage train got swept into the mud by a surge in the tide near Wisbech, which isn't far from Weldelph, but nobody has ever found them.

'Idiots,' he said. 'Idiots come along and dig holes everywhere but they never find anything—because there's nothing to be found.'

She pouted and called him unromantic—'just like the hard, cruel business man you are.'

He wagged his finger at her across the table. 'If I happened to act for Joshua Lovegrove and had his accounts in my office over there, you would be across the bridge like a shot wanting to see them. That's one

50

book you'd love to bury your pretty nose in.'

'You'd never let me. You're so secretive about your silly old books.'

The sunlight glinted on the coffee pot and made it look like a little blue and white pagoda. As she reached to tilt it, she saw a person on the pavement below. It was quite easy to tell that she knew she made a perfect picture, framed by the window, and she poured to bring it to life.

Lacey smiled. 'Secretive, am I?'

'Abominably,' said Nina. 'You keep me in the dark about everything.'

'Far from everything, my love, I can let you into a secret at this very moment.'

There was a composure about him now that she appreciated. It gave him such a presence. She remained silent, allowing him to pace what he had to say.

'Joshua Lovegrove doesn't know it yet, but there may be treasure for him in King John's Lakes after all. They may have a much higher saleable value than such a marshy bit of land is worth. Some people are even considering making him an offer.'

She said all of this, almost word for word, in court when the scandal came into the open. She even went to the extent of telling everybody in court that he stood up and buttoned his jacket and refused to say any more. It was just as well he didn't, because he was the man in the dock for trying to cheat old Josh out of his land. She was making out how nice he was, how open and honest in everything he did, which was why she was gushing and giving everything away. She never mentioned how underhand he was about the grasshopper, but this may have been because she didn't notice anything so unimportant.

9 Harry and Mozart

Crazy pictures of a grasshopper as big as a horse were never going to have much effect on Harry's father, even though they appealed to Harry. Mr Julian Green is typical Weldelph—he only goes for pictures he can understand.

I like Harry's mother, though. She's the sort of person who won't say something is bad just because she can't make head or tail of it; what she'll do is make a bit of a joke about being ignorant. I remember Harry telling me what happened when that film about Mozart, *Amadeus*, was going to be on telly and there were loads of trailers all showing that bit where Mozart farts.

'Every time I turn the telly on,' said his mother, 'there it is.'

'Yes,' said Harry. 'You'd think that's all there was.'

'Amadeus! Who'd wish a name like that on a child? And then for him to do that.' She has a way of clicking her tongue and turning her eyes up.

'It's nothing like him,' said Harry.

'You're just a little phoney like the rest, Harold Green. Are you trying to tell me Mozart didn't? And you needn't screw up your face like that. What is it that makes you so goodie-goodie lately? You in love or something?'

She wore tight jeans and a checked shirt. When she was dressed like that, an imitation man pretending to be a feminist, Harry's father always said she was nicely packaged.

'When does Dad come home?' he asked.

When she laughs it pushes her cheeks up and slits her

eyes. 'Change the subject,' she chanted. 'That's you all over.'

'If that's the way you want it.' He had taken off his jacket, but he still wore his tie. He loosened it. 'Mozart did, Shakespeare did, so did Elvis.'

'Which one—Presley or . . . ?' She thrust her head forward, waiting for him to fill in the missing name. She is a blonde but she has fairer streaks that are like speed lines sweeping back from her blunt face. She always seems in a hurry. 'Come on, Clever Dick, don't tell me you don't know there was more than one Elvis.'

Once, when he was very young, Harry had gazed into her light grey eyes with little black dots in the centre, and then had told her they were just like frog spawn. He stared at her now and said it again.

She flapped a hand at his head but he caught her by the wrist. 'You didn't know,' she said. 'You're so high and mighty you didn't know there was more than one Elvis.'

'Yes, I did.'

'No, you didn't.'

'It just slipped my mind. I'm not like some people—I don't listen to Radio One all day.'

'Better than watching Mozart's bum.'

He released her, and she went out of the living room, leaving him staring through the glass doors into the winter garden. Elvis Costello. Now it came back to him. But too late, like many other things. Beyond the patio, the blue lining of the empty pool was exposed. Some patches had flaked like the inside wall of a derelict house. The Costello poster was rolled up in the corner of his room. Laurie Anderson had taken over. And Mozart.

Sounds from outside made the muscles of his chest tighten. It was always the same when he heard the tyres of his father's car roll into the drive and then the dying flutter of the engine. For a full beat there was silence, then the clunk of the door mingled with the brilliant clatter of cutlery from the kitchen and his mother's voice calling. He went through.

If you say 'Elizabeth Avenue' to anyone in Weldelph they'll know straight away you're talking about money. For instance, even the kitchen in Harry's house is larger than Trigger Harris's living room. In Trigger's house the tables are stacked to the corners with bread bins, books, letters and toasters, and cupboard doors won't close—but if you live in Elizabeth Avenue there's room to move. Charlotte is right—Harry's a rich kid, compared to most. Which is maybe why, in the end, he told me such a lot about what happened. It just spilled out, every detail. If you're rich you don't need to protect yourself—you've got money to fall back on.

'I saw you with a girl last night,' said his father, who was eating before Harry sat down. 'You never saw me, though.'

'And he told me,' said his mother, pouring tea for his father, 'that he was going to a lecture.'

Harry said nothing.

'She's a looker, I reckon.' His father chewed and drank. 'Bit on the broad side.'

'Not anorexic.' His mother winked at Harry. 'But maybe she ought to eat a bit more salad, like me.'

'Hold it a minute, Roz.' His father held up his knife. 'He hasn't told us who she is yet.'

'I didn't see you.' Harry looked directly at him. 'Where were you last night?'

His father ceased chewing and regarded him for a long moment before he said, 'I'm not obliged to tell you anything, my son.' He waited until Harry's eyes fell, and then he began to hum to himself as he resumed eating.

Roz Green was nervous. Her husband was used to getting his own way. People answered when he asked a question. 'Well, I know where *you* were,' she said to him. 'You're not going to tell me Harry was in the pub

54

as well.' She herself did not stop eating, cutting her food into tiny fragments and feeding her grin with short, jerky movements. She turned to her son. 'Were you?'

It was the night of the grasshopper picture, so Harry had been in no pub. He said so.

Mr Julian Green is broad, like Harry, but he carries a lot more muscle, so when he takes off his jacket his white shirt bulges like a pillow. You can see black hair when he undoes the top button, and it also grows in his ears, but his bald head is as smooth as a kid glove. He's no Julian to look at, and he doesn't sound like one, either.

'There's no secret about what I do,' he said to Harry's mother. 'I was just on my way to have a quiet bevvy in my usual place last night, when who should I see walking across the market place but young mastermind and this bird he won't tell us about.'

Harry watched his father's anger swelling with each word, and he broke in quickly, trying to head it off. 'I wanted to ask you something,' he said.

His father resumed eating, but now his large, dark eyes looked up. 'I thought I was asking *you* something,' he said.

Harry put down his knife and fork and pushed his chair back. It was far too big a gesture, and his mouth had gone dry. 'I thought it was clear I wasn't going to give you an answer.'

His father, even in winter, has a tan. The muscles of his brown face ceased chewing.

Harry heard the despicable hoarseness in his own voice that gave away his fear. 'And she isn't a bird,' he said.

His father's luminous eyes are as black as grapes. He allowed their stare to rest on his son until Harry saw the hardness within, and he began to chew again. 'Not a bird,' he said. 'Is that so?'

Harry stood up.

55

'Eat your food.'

'No.'

The bald head took so long to tilt back that Harry thought his father had heard nothing. But then, very slowly, the face was raised so that the eyes, suddenly expressionless, rested on him, and his father belched.

'You two!' Roz Green seized the moment to put her voice between them. 'Stop squabbling like a couple of kids. And you,' she grabbed Harry by the arm, 'you sit down and eat your dinner.'

'Lunch,' he said, and the feebleness of his defiance made his eyes prick with shameful tears. She had seen he was still afraid of the thick arms and heavy hands on the other side of the table.

'Lunch, then,' she said. 'Just don't stand there like a spare at a wedding. Sit down.' She saw him hesitate. 'What was it you wanted to ask your father?'

'It doesn't matter. He wouldn't agree anyway.'

'Try me.' It was unexpected, and it was humiliating. His father knew that Harry's defiance had evaporated and he did not even bother to look up from his plate. 'Try me.'

Harry stood where he was and grimaced down at the bald head. It was an outward show of bravery for his mother to see. 'You wouldn't want anybody rummaging among the old stock in your warehouse,' he said.

'You're dead right there, son.'

'Especially a friend of mine.'

His father looked up, grinning. 'Female? Your female friend?'

'No. Male. And old. Very old.' Each word pumped up his anger, pushing fear aside. 'And somebody you wouldn't want to know. You despise him.' He had circled the table and was just near the door, his exit line ready. 'Just in case you want to know, it's old Josh Lovegrove.'

He opened the door but he was not quick enough. His

56

father was on his feet in front of him, and the door slammed shut.

'Who did you say?'

Not for a long time had he been close enough to feel his father's warmth. He felt it now; the body heat of a large animal. And one surprise. Their eyes were level. Until that instant he had always thought of himself as having to look upwards into his father's face.

'Who did you say!'

'Old Josh Lovegrove.'

Their eyes held. And now you can hit me if it pleases you, Harry thought, but I'll tell you one more thing. 'I like him,' he said. 'Old Josh is a friend of mine.'

There was no blow. The thick fingers that were splayed against the door slid away.

'Why didn't you say it was him?' His father stepped back and made a gesture indicating that his son should sit down; please. 'You never said it was old Lovegrove.'

'You never asked.'

'Don't look so bombed out, mate. Of course I never asked. You knock around with some peculiar bloody people—that loony with the bike, what's-his-name?'

Trigger Harris. But Harry said nothing. He reached for the door handle.

'Hold it!' His father gestured vaguely to take the sting out of the order. Something had changed. 'Look, what I mean is you treat me and your mother as though we're a couple of yobs, which you only have to look at this house and pool and everything to see we're not. So we think you mix with some pretty funny people. Fair's fair.'

'Birds,' said Harry.

'I'm not talking about birds. I don't give a monkey's about birds.'

'Thank you very much,' said his wife.

'You know what I mean, Roz. It's them others. Some of 'em.'

Roz turned to her son. 'Your father's right,' she said. 'You'd think we couldn't read or something, the way you talk to us sometimes.'

Harry remained silent. He'd never said they *couldn't* read; just that they never did.

'Anyway,' his father had lost patience with explanations, 'what does old Josh want? I'll take a bet it's something bloody batty.'

'American Gut,' said Harry, and watched them both laugh.

10 Hexagon Square

If Harry's father had paid more attention to his son and the grasshopper he would have saved himself a lot of trouble. He never gave Harry credit for having much sense and was always going on at him for the friends he kept—people like Trigger Harris; and me, I suppose—because we don't have our feet firmly on the ground which, according to Mr Julian Green, is the only place for feet. Personally, if I can fly, I will.

There was a fortune staring Julian Green in the face, and all he did was laugh at it. But even now you can't blame him, in a way, for not following up the clues to the grasshopper, because it must have seemed just something pretty stupid his son was involved in, and he had other things on his mind. He was at war. He wanted to alter his warehouse, and the council wouldn't let him. He said they were ruining his business.

Harold Green and Son's warehouse is just over the bridge in Hexagon Square, which isn't a square, and isn't a hexagon either. It's a triangle, where they still hold a market once a week, and it got its name from the Hexagon Church. The church had six pinnacles and you

58

used to be able to see it from miles away across the fens, until they pulled it down. My father's got a phrase for that, as he has for most things—he says it's civic vandalism, and he reckons Weldelph is still at it. He and my mother are really uptight about it, so when I heard Harry's father one day say that getting rid of the old Hexagon was a bloody good idea, it suddenly hit me that there was part of Weldelph I knew nothing about. I mean, I was sure everybody thought it was a pity you couldn't any longer sit watching a cricket match and see the six spires over the elms, but that was my mistake.

'They get rid of one useless old monstrosity,' said Julian Green, 'but they won't let me rip out the front of my warehouse so as I can bring it up to date.'

I heard him say it because Harry's house is a bit open plan and his father's voice carries. We were in the kitchen about a mile away. Harry's mother said, 'It's those little windows along the front, Julian. Everybody reckons they've got a lot of charm.'

'I'll run my bloody Volvo into them one night, then see what charm they've got.'

Harry raised his eyebrows at me. He was embarrassed because my parents were making a bit of a noise about things like that. He got up to close the kitchen door, but I did hear his mother say, 'You've got mates on the council, Julian, so why don't you get them to do something about it?' And then just before the door was shut I heard Mr Lacey Lockyer's name mentioned.

I wish I had heard a bit more, because it must have been just about that time that Lacey Lockyer was getting his hooks into Harry's father and making Julian Green do his dirty work for him. Not that they weren't about as bad as each other. I mean Julian Green *did* want to buy King John's Lakes from Josh Lovegrove without telling old Josh he had plans to make a lot of money from the Lakes. Lacey Lockyer was worse, if anything. He was going to fiddle the plans through the council without letting anyone know he had put most of the money into it as well. That's what landed him in court. Harry didn't know what was happening. All he wanted to know about was American Gut.

Although none of them knew it, American Gut was the clue to everything. Harry guessed the gut might bring him closer to the grasshopper, whatever that really was, but his father was using it as a kind of bribe. Anyway, because of the court case, everybody now knows what the two men said to each other in Julian Green's office next day.

'American Gut!' said Julian Green. 'What the hell my boy has been up to with the old fool I'm damned if I know, but if old Josh Lovegrove wants American Gut he can have American Gut—by the ton if I've got it.'

'Let's hope you have, Julian,' said Lacey Lockyer.

'And I don't even know what it looks like! It goes back to my grandfather's day and they used it like rope, or like catgut, sheep gut, elephant gut—I don't know, but they used it in some sorts of machinery because it was elastic and tough, or so they tell me. All I know is that my grandfather used to sell the stuff and he never threw anything away. Nor did my old man, so there might be some of it still laying about somewhere upstairs.'

'You haven't been to look?'

'My boy only sprung it on me yesterday. First useful thing he's done in the whole of his born days, little does he know it.'

Lacey Lockyer watched him smile and then said, 'You'll give old Lovegrove the run of the premises?'

'That's the idea, Lacey. Get old Josh so obligated to me, and to my boy, that he'll have to *listen* to me at least. And I don't reckon he can refuse the kind of offer we are going to make.'

In court, Lacey Lockyer denied that he had anything to do with the offer; he said it was entirely Julian

Green's idea, but they do agree that their discussion ended there because Lacey Lockyer, looking out of the office window, saw Harry coming across the square towards the warehouse. Charlotte was with him, which was never mentioned, but it was a surprise to both of them. Harry's father realized she was even prettier than he had thought; and Lacey Lockyer already had cause to know exactly who she was.

11 The Outsider

Harry knew he was taking a risk in bringing Charlotte to the warehouse to help in the search for American Gut. He could never tell what his father's mood would be, especially with one of Harry's friends, and especially a girl. As it happened, Julian Green wasn't the one that Charlotte had to worry about, although he frightened her when she first saw him.

She hadn't realized how large Harry's father was until she saw him standing behind the trade counter. With the recesses of the warehouse stretching away into the dimness behind him, he loomed over the counter, his hands spread wide, like a massive guardian at the mouth of a cave. His lair had the warehouse smell of tar and oil, and the wooden floor was dusty and uneven. She would have stumbled if Harry had not touched her arm.

Mr Green was lifting the heavy flap of the counter and Harry was introducing her, but saying too much, as though he had to justify bringing her there. He said she was somebody who was interested in old Josh Lovegrove and the history of Weldelph and all that kind of thing, so he'd brought her along and hoped his father didn't mind.

61

Julian Green didn't mind at all. That was the trouble. His hand rested on her waist as he showed her through to his office. Just to look at her you'd know that Charlotte must have had men doing this before, but she told me later that with Julian Green's hairy hand on her hip she felt about as safe as walking side by side with a bear. And the fact that the bear was her boyfriend's father made it worse.

She was glad when he showed her to a chair, but before she could sit down she saw there was another man in the office. She liked him better. He was smaller than Julian Green, for one thing, and also he was darkly handsome and very polite. He shook her hand and said, 'I'm pleased to meet you, Miss Bush.'

It surprised her that he knew her name without being told, and it seemed to take Julian Green unawares as well. 'You've got the advantage of me, Lacey,' he said. 'You know her already.'

'In a sense.'

'In a sense.' Julian Green smiled at Harry. 'I like that, *in a sense*. That's a cautious man talking, a good business man.'

Harry had nothing to say. He was too much aware of the crude contrast his father made to the quiet consultant. Lacey Lockyer had resumed his seat, and his smooth face was placid.

There was a silence. It was imposed by Lacey Lockyer. He appeared to be thinking intensely, and although all he did was turn his head away, Charlotte saw that it curbed Mr Green's bluster even in his own office. They all waited, and when eventually he spoke nobody quite understood what he meant.

'Tell me, Julian,' he said, 'who is to accompany our visitor when he arrives?' Harry's father looked blank until Lacey Lockyer gave him a little more to go on, but he still left Charlotte feeling he did not want anybody else to understand him. 'When our friend from out of town arrives,' he said, 'and goes to look through your old stock, who is to accompany him?'

'Go upstairs with old Josh, you mean?' Harry's father let it out of the bag.

'I do.' The words chopped him off. 'Who is to accompany him upstairs to seek ... To seek what he hopes to find?'

'Well ...' Julian Green was beginning to get the message that he should not say too much in front of a stranger. Charlotte knew that she was the odd one out, and she felt more of an outsider still when Julian Green said, 'Well, Harry will go with him, I suppose.' No mention of Charlotte herself.

'I see.'

'And me, of course,' added Julian Green.

There was a pause. Nobody looked at Charlotte until Harry gave a nervous cough. It was obvious that he was about to say that she would also help in the search, but he didn't get the chance; Lacey Lockyer interrupted him by turning towards her.

'How is your brother, Miss Bush?'

She will never forget the long moment his eyes rested on her and how she felt herself forced to return his stare. She gazed at him intently simply because it drove every other thought out of her mind. There was something pressing forward that she did not want to know. But her silence could not last for ever, and he asked her again about her brother.

'Derek?' Her voice had a little girl's panic. He nodded, and she could no longer keep her mind closed. She knew Lacey Lockyer. The court room came back to her, and the three magistrates in a row facing her brother. Lacey Lockyer had been one of them; the harmless one who never said anything.

'Derek's at home at the moment,' she said.

'Not at work?'

'Yes.' Then she corrected herself. 'Well, no.'

63

'I see.' The dark eyes looked down briefly, and were then raised to Harry's father. 'Miss Bush's elder brother had a misfortune, Julian. We met when I was in another place.'

'Where was that, Lacey?' Julian Green had not understood.

The consultant spoke again, repeating his words. 'I was sitting,' he said deliberately, 'in another place.'

Then, at last, it dawned on Julian Green. Mr Lacey Lockyer, magistrate. With this girl's brother in front of him.

Harry saw his father turn away, raising one hand to rub the back of his neck as he stepped behind his desk and sat down. Then he lay back, tapped his fingers like a piano player, stopped suddenly and looked straight at Charlotte. In silence.

Harry's first treachery began there. He was slow to understand, even when Charlotte suddenly stood up.

'I'm sorry, Harry,' she said. 'I forgot. I promised . . .' She was going to say she had to meet someone, but the words would not come. She made straight for the door and he sat where he was and watched her. He did not stir.

Later, he told himself that she had moved so quickly he had been bewildered, but he knew this was not true. Then he blamed himself for cowardice, of being afraid to risk his father's anger. The truth was even more shameful than that. He had been brought to heel. The magistrate and his father had reminded him who he was. He was one of their sort. The girl had a brother who went to prison. She was the other part of Weldelph. When the choice came, Harry had stayed with his own kind and watched her driven out.

To give him his due, he did get to his feet as the door closed behind her, but by then it was too late. And quite suddenly he was able to justify himself. He caught a glimpse of Josh Lovegrove crossing the square and remembered the purpose of his visit to the warehouse. The search for American Gut. He had to stay to help. He would explain it all to Charlotte later—so he let her go, and his betrayal was complete.

12 A Fist on the Desk

When his father went out of the office to meet old Josh, Harry was left alone with Lacey Lockyer. He was cornered. Later, when he could bear to talk about it, he admitted he could feel himself coming to his senses. He should never have deserted Charlotte, but now it was too late. His anger, mainly with himself, began to boil. He put his head down and shook it, just like a bull, and when he looked up he could see that Lacey Lockyer knew that trouble was brewing. Harry wanted to charge and gore the neat grey suit and the soft underbelly of the waistcoat. But Lacey Lockyer was too cunning for him.

'One of the prettiest girls in Weldelph,' he said. 'Such a shame.'

Harry's head jerked up, still like a young bull, and Lacey Lockyer goaded him.

'I don't know what she sees in you, Harry, but you must have something.'

A grunt. The dart of flattery had gone home. Now he planted another.

'An extremely intelligent girl, too. I could tell that she impressed your father.'

A snort and a twist of the head. Lacey Lockyer trailed his cape.

'But she has her misfortunes—as I believe I hinted.'

'You did,' said Harry. 'You certainly did.'

It was a short charge, and the consultant did not flinch. 'You already knew about her brother, of course,' he said.

A snort and a glare.

'But I'm afraid your father knows of his misdemeanours, too. Because I practically spelled it out to him.'

It was daring cape work to be so open, but it succeeded. He was running rings around Harry.

'And did *you* notice how your father shrugged it off as a matter of no consequence? Without so much as uttering a single word? He remained silent—when the one thing I admire in your father above all else is his utter frankness. His *brutal* frankness, in fact.'

It was a diversionary swing and again raised the young bull's head and held it there.

'If your father had the slightest animosity towards your charming girlfriend she would certainly have been the first to know.'

Lacey Lockyer's timing was perfect. The door opened. Now was the moment of truth.

'Ah, Julian, we have just been discussing you. Isn't that so, Harry?'

Harry's glance stabbed at his father, and the consultant paused. In that moment of silence, Harry's head swung first one way and then the other, and then he gave up. He looked away, and the smooth face smiled.

'We were saying, Julian, how sympathetic you were to the young lady and how much we admired you for it.'

Harry's head was bowed. The consultant gave him no chance to raise it. He turned his back on him and spoke louder so that old Josh, who was lingering outside, could hear him.

'Mr Lovegrove,' he said, 'I warn you to beware of this man Julian Green—he is far too susceptible to female charms.'

Charlotte could have told him that, but now it was Josh's turn to be bewildered. 'You mean the young lady who just went out?' he asked, and then he turned towards Julian Green. 'Please to forgive the wrong impression, but I thought she was your daughtuar.'

Angry as he was, Harry remembered that this very nearly made the consultant smile, and Lacey Lockyer changed the subject to control his face. 'King John's Lakes must be frozen over, Mr Lovegrove.'

'In this weathuar,' Josh agreed, 'solid.'

Lacey Lockyer did not laugh, but he had to struggle to bring the chocolate tone back to his voice. 'Not a very comfortable place to live, I imagine.'

'Your imagination,' said Josh, 'is in accordance with the facts.'

There was a wateriness in Lacey Lockyer's eyes as he said, 'Some discomfort is inevitable with older properties.'

'And railway carriages,' said Josh.

'Yes, indeed. It is bitter weather for travelling.'

'No,' said Josh. 'I inhabit one. A railway carriage is a difficult structuar to keep warm—because of its length. It can be as clammy as a serpuent.'

It was when his father began to sympathize with old Josh's plight, living alone in an old railway carriage out in the wilds, that Harry first began to sense that there was more to it than a desire to help. His father laid it on too thick, and very soon was suggesting that old Josh should sell up and move into town.

'There are some nice little properties close to the centre,' he said. 'Wouldn't mind one myself.' This was a lie. Harry very well knew his father would never move to a smaller house. But Julian Green laughed and leant forward to rest both elbows on his desk. 'If I could afford it,' he said.

'That is the fly in the honey pot,' Josh agreed. 'Money is in short supply.'

Harry watched as they both shook their heads. The little man was smiling like a simpleton who believed himself sharp-witted, and Harry began to see what was happening. He himself was not the only one who was being manipulated. Now the consultant was joining in. He smoothly pointed out that Josh was already a man of property—he owned King John's Lakes.

This made Julian Green laugh again. 'A bit of marshland isn't exactly what most people would call *property*,' he said. 'You can't make a living off of it.'

The consultant, his eyes looking down at his knee, made no reply.

'Come on, Lacey, *you* know and *I* know that even if he sold up everything he wouldn't have enough for one of them nice little places. You don't mind me saying that, do you, Josh old friend?'

Josh did not mind in the least.

Lacey Lockyer smoothed one trouser leg. 'That's where I think you're wrong again, Julian. There is a market for land to be developed.'

'But not *marshland*, Lacey. You can't develop that.'

'Who knows?' The grey shoulders shrugged, hardly interested, but Harry was fascinated. He saw what they were doing. He saw his father and the smooth consultant going to work on the little man who sat twiddling his cane between his legs and had no idea what was happening. First they said his land wasn't worth much, then they said it might be, and eventually they got into an argument over it just as though old Josh wasn't there.

You have to give Harry credit for seeing what was happening, especially as his own father was one of the culprits, and he wanted to stop it but he could hardly accuse his father then and there. He was helpless, even when it came to the point of Julian Green making an offer to buy the land himself. It was a ridiculous joke, or seemed so, until Lacey Lockyer took him seriously and said he wasn't offering enough.

'All right, I'll put it up a couple of thou.' His father really did sound indignant.

'Not nearly enough, Julian.'

'Five, then.'

The consultant shook his head.

'Ten.' The auction had become serious, and suddenly Harry found he could stand it no longer.

'Dad,' he said. 'It's getting dark.'

His father seemed to come out of a daydream. 'So what?' he said. 'I don't get you.'

'We won't be able to see our way up the stairs if we wait much longer.' But his father still did not understand. 'American Gut,' said Harry. 'Remember?'

'Well why don't you just sod off and look for it yourself? You're clogging up the works down here.' Temper had brought his eyebrows together. 'Go on, clear off.'

But the outburst had alarmed old Josh who was on his feet, apologizing. He feared he had taken up too much of their time; they were busy men and his own affairs were trifling and of no consequence; he would be on his way now; terribly sorry to have caused such trouble; good afternoon.

Harry watched his father, fighting to overcome his fury, come smiling around his desk to prevent the little man wind any more of his scarf around his neck. 'You didn't take that seriously, did you, Joshua old mate? Me and my boy are always sounding off at each other. We've got this thing going, father and son, know what I mean? Ain't that so, Harry boy?'

'Whatever you say, Father.'

'See what I mean? Sarcasm from him. And I chuck in a bit of abuse. We love it.' His smile showed all his teeth. 'So just you be off, Harry boy, and rootle about upstairs to your heart's content.' His smile faded as Josh also headed for the door, but he forced it to return. 'So you're going with him are you, Josh? By all means, be my guest. I'm always ready to oblige a fellow business man, old friend.'

Harry, as he closed the door behind himself and the

69

old man, listened for sounds from the office. It was so silent it could have been empty. Then there was a thud like a fist coming down on the desk.

13 Derek's Sister

Money and looks have a lot in common. Charlotte's attitude towards her looks is a bit like my father's way with money. He doesn't give a damn. With her eyes, that nose and that perfect mouth Charlotte has the prettiest face in Weldelph, but she doesn't care. She really doesn't. And that makes her even prettier. I wish that not caring about money made my father richer. The only time he ever thinks about money is when he's broke—and this is like Charlotte as well. She's only aware of the way she looks when she thinks she's ugly.

She was sure of it when she ran away from the warehouse. Lacey Lockyer began it by reminding everybody that her brother had been to prison. Derek Bush isn't even a very big crook—he gets caught too often—and he's more than twice her age, so there's such a big gap she shouldn't let it bother her. But Lacey Lockyer let her know that Weldelph had different ideas. She was tainted, and she ran. She had left the square and was crossing the bridge before she looked back. There was no sign of Harry.

She stood where she was and allowed the wind, as it came wolfing up the channel, to bite moisture from her eyes. The tide was pushing inland and the river was high and fat with mud. Girls died in that.

She waited at the end of the bridge until the traffic was halted by the lights and then she crossed the road. Her tears now were genuine. She had not dared to step

70

in front of a car. The thought of her own face, gone chalk white, her skin broken, had halted her.

But girls did die. They were found in fields with their skirts up and their troubles ended.

She was ugly. She knew it. That quiet, dark man had made her ugliness show. Bit by bit he had put her back into the place where she belonged; the house with the bike against the front window; the back yard with the tin bath hanging on the wall beside the lavatory door. And prison. Derek's prison had a long, dusty tongue that reached out and touched her.

Her clothes did not fit, and she moved awkwardly inside them. They were part of her ugliness. Nothing about her had been enough to draw Harry from his father's office.

She stopped in front of a photographer's shop window and saw her ghost in the glass. She was simplified and made pure. And the framed brides beyond the glass were images of purity. This was what girls should be made of. Their heads were haloed in white and they supported their bosoms on banks of flowers, but she did not belong with them. She did not belong anywhere. Suddenly the brides disgusted her. They smirked in monotonous rows. They were identical. They were a graveyard. She turned her back on them and shuddered, shaking herself free of their sickly icing sugar.

The pleasure did not last. Harry had let her go. It was getting dark and became darker still as Ely Crescent closed in and she spoke aloud, not caring if anyone overheard. 'He heard that man say things about me, and he let me go.'

She gazed down at the toes of her shoes as they showed themselves one after the other, and she did not see the curator until it was too late. He was at the top of the museum steps smiling down at her.

'Can you spare me a moment?' he said. His long legs

brought him swiftly down the steps and she barely had time to knuckle away some of the tears. 'I saw you from afar,' he said.

'It's the cold wind. It's making me cry.'

'I watched you because I wish to speak to you.'

'I look awful.'

'If this is awful,' he said, 'I tremble to think what your smile would do.'

A smile would press more tears from her eyes. She turned away.

He had remembered her name. 'Miss Bush,' he said, 'may we have words?' He waited until she nodded, still not looking at him. 'But not on the frozen steps of Weldelph Museum and Literary Society! I have the necessities for coffee in my room—' he corrected himself '—in my *office*. I do not seek to lure you to my private apartments.' He turned to allow her to precede him up the steps. 'Unless, of course, you are willing to be lured.'

'I don't care.'

He halted so suddenly that she was two steps above him before she knew it. 'In that case, we had best go no further.'

A few minutes ago, the consultant's stare had driven her out into the cold. Equally dark eyes were on her now, but a different game was being played. 'Why should I care?' she said. He could not harm her more than she had been harmed already. She laughed, and he laughed with her.

'If there be no restraint on your part,' he said, 'I cannot answer for the consequences.'

'Consequences? You are making a mockery of a poor girl.'

'Girl.' He advanced a step, which put his head on a level with hers. 'Girl is a lovely word. And I do not mock.'

But he had mocked her out of the word; stripped her

out of girl. She was suddenly older than herself, his equal in age, able to match him word for word. The shock of it sobered her.

'What is it you want to talk to me about?' she said.

'It's about the other night.' He also had become formal, no longer joking. 'That stupid lecture I gave. You seemed to have something to tell me.'

'Did I? I don't remember.' To prevent her eyes from meeting his, she went ahead of him up the steps.

The glass panel of the door shivered as he let her into the museum's foyer, and then he opened a heavy door set deep in an alcove and showed her into a room where an old gas fire whimpered under a marble mantel.

'I'm afraid we are quite alone,' he said. 'I do apologize, but you can sit in yonder window and call for help from passers-by if need be.'

He was boyish now and too elaborate. She ignored what he was saying and walked sedately past the two desks in the room and stood beside the fire.

'Please take a seat.' He had not advanced with her but remained in the corner by the door where a kettle and china mugs stood on a tray. 'Black or white?'

She told him, and while his back was turned she took out a handkerchief and wiped her eyes and nose. There was a little mirror on the desk nearest to her and she stooped to see herself. This time the glass did not purify. She saw what she was. Her eyes were swollen and her face looked damaged. There was even a straggle of hair across her forehead. She was Derek's sister.

'Please don't think that's my mirror.' Hugh Beamish had turned round. 'My vanity does not go that far. That's Mrs Frost's desk. She's supposed to work for me but she knows too much; far, far too much, and she terrifies me. She'd make an admirable chaperone for you, but I'm afraid she's only part-time—part-time chaperone to me, that is.'

Charlotte took the mug he offered her without saying

a word and he, seeing that her mood had changed again, became less flippant.

'What I wanted to ask you about was that absurd photograph. The man-sized grasshopper. People seemed ridiculously interested in it, and I thought you wanted to say something—not that you were ridiculous, of course.' His voice was telling her, however, that she was not to feel threatened. He had ceased being interested in the girl. Now he was the curator. 'Actually I wasn't quite sure whether it was you who had the information or your boyfriend.'

'He's not my boyfriend.' It was easy to say. 'He's not my boyfriend at all. In fact he despises me.'

'He can't do that! That's not possible, Miss Bush.'

She had seen it done in plays. 'Charlotte,' she said. It was surprisingly easy, and she did not even blush.

Harry had been driven from her mind, but the grasshopper was a link between them that had been growing stronger from the moment she left the warehouse. Neither knew it. Harry was busy seeking some strange substance with an old man in his father's warehouse, while in the museum Charlotte sat in a swivel chair with her toes towards the fire and both hands clutching her coffee mug. 'All I need,' she said, 'is a blanket round my shoulders and I'd look like the survivor of a disaster.'

'What disaster? Has it been that bad?' asked Hugh Beamish.

'Bad enough. But I'm not going to tell *you* about it.' She risked looking sideways at him, knowing that the firelight would gleam in her eyes. He had full lips for such a thin face and, when he was not attempting to be amusing, his features were naturally solemn. The gas flames sighed and popped and gave out a flickering light that made him appear like some silent fur trapper at his camp fire.

'I've told you enough already,' she said. Secrets had spilled from her—she had told him of Joshua

74

Lovegrove's handbill of the grasshopper, and even the fact that Harry and Josh were at this moment in the warehouse searching for something they had seen in an old catalogue.

'Charlotte,' said Hugh Beamish, 'this stuff that old Josh is after, whatever it is, why is it so important?'

'Harry Green didn't tell me much,' she said. 'All I know is that Mr Lovegrove needs it to make some machinery work. But he's crazy. Both of them are.'

And she had been stupid, too, she thought, when she was one of them. But that was already in the past. Now she was different.

'I'd like some more coffee,' she said. 'Please, Hugh.'

Harry and Josh had climbed five flights of wooden stairs. At this height there was more light from the setting sun than in the floors below. It streamed in horizontally through the barred windows, deepening the shadows but in places cutting long corridors of pink light between the crowded islands of boxes and crates and farm tackle stacked on the wide floor.

'I smell ships,' said Josh. 'Hemp and tar.' He sniffed. 'I am about to follow my nose, young felluar,' and he moved swiftly into an alleyway, his cane tapping and his coat hem sweeping up dust to sparkle in the pink evening light each time he stooped to inspect something.

PART THREE

14 Derek and the Milkman

Blame Charlotte. She told me a lot about her brother, and what happened did happen. She said so.

The Cortina was tired. It rubbed gently into the kerb and sighed to rest.

'I wouldn't do anything to harm that kid, you know that,' said Derek Bush.

'There was a bit of a jolt there,' said the milkman. 'I think one of your shockers has gone.'

'It's the roads, Ted, there's no upkeep. I wouldn't do anything against her. Never have.'

'I noticed your door sills has both gone,' said the milkman. 'Poke your finger through.'

'They always go there, but it ain't a structural defect. The car ain't going to fold in two like a bloody shut-knife.'

The milkman had his peaked cap in his lap. He tapped cigarette ash onto its flat top. 'Didn't suppose it would,' he said. 'What happened to your ash tray?'

'I got it, don't worry about that. It's in the boot.' Derek Bush was a short man, and plump, and he did not look comfortable leaning forward with his forearm curved around the top of the steering wheel. His own ash fell to the rubber mat. 'I treat her like I would my own sister,' he said. 'Well I suppose that's natural, as that's what she is. But when that Mr Lockyer called me into his office this morning and told me he knew her, I did wonder if the little cow had got into some kind of trouble, know what I mean ?'

77

'Well, you would,' said the milkman, 'seeing as who he is.'

'On the bench and that.' It was cold in the car but Derek was sweating.

'And seeing as who you are,' said the milkman. 'Your heater don't work, I notice.'

'Air lock, but I never bother about it. The engine keeps the ambient temperature just about right, are you wi' me? You could've knocked me down when he said she was a nice girl—no, I tell a lie; his words were "a very charming young lady who should be cherished." He's got that way of speaking—cherished—you'd hardly believe he was a Weldelph boy. He's all right is Mr Lockyer. A bit slippery and cherishy, but all right, if you follow me. You always know where you are with a bugger like that.'

'The wife is a very chilly person in a car,' said Ted. 'Cold-blooded. Definitely. So what was it he had you in for?'

'Charity. Oh sod this cigarette!' The end had fallen off into his grey gaberdine lap. 'Even fags has got bleeding built-in obsolescence nowadays.' He pounded at his coat to put out the smouldering tip. 'Mr Lockyer said he wanted to help me out a bit, and do somebody else a good turn at the same time.'

'Who else would that be?' said the milkman.

'I thought he was referring to my supervisor.' Derek's stubby fingers wheedled another cigarette out of the packet and into the glistening red of his face.

'That the gaffer of your project?' The milkman suddenly became loquacious. 'Community work, ain't it? You got to do so many hours for the community, that's what it said when your case come up in the paper. You was lucky to get that. Doin' up kitchens for old ladies, you tell me—now the weather's too bad for gardenin'. That the gaffer you mean?'

'Yeh.' Derek spoke shortly, trying to stop him. 'That's the one.'

'Supposed to help learn you a trade while you're doing it, that right?'

'Yes, Ted, but . . .'

'Well why don't you have a look at this motor and do the rust and a paint job before you flog it? Makes all the difference, paint.'

'Well, listen, Ted, I went to see this Mr Lockyer and he didn't want to know nothing about community work, nor my bloody supervisor as it turns out. "Nothing to do with me, Mr Bush, I've asked you to come here on another matter entirely".'

'That's him talking to you, is it? That's what he said to you? In his office?'

'Listen, Ted. He started talking to me about a different matter entirely, didn't he?'

'If you say so,' said the milkman, 'but . . .'

'I do say so, Ted. And what he said was very interesting. Very interesting indeed. You know old Josh Lovegrove, don't you? You don't have to answer because I know you do. Everyone does. It was just a rhetorical question asking you that. Everyone who lives in Weldelph knows him.'

'I know old Josh.' The milkman had become laconic again. 'There's a hell of a fug in here. Do the ventilator work?'

'You ever hear of ventilators that don't bloody work? They're only a little bloody hole through the bloody bodywork. When we're *moving* they bloody near blow your stupid head off.'

'I was only askin',' said the milkman.

Derek Bush had to pause to gather himself. He shut his eyes and pinched the bridge of his nose. 'Oh bloody hell where was I? Don't answer . . . I know, I know.' He took a breath. 'Mr Lockyer said he was taking a personal interest in my case. He said he'd heard in a roundabout kind of way that my lovely young sister had got to know some guy at the museum.'

'Museum?' said Ted. 'Is that the one in Ely Crescent?'

'There's only one museum in Weldelph, Ted. Weldelph Museum it's called.'

'That's the one I meant,' said Ted.

'Seemingly,' said Derek steadily, 'my little sister had got to know the guy who runs it, and I'm given to understand that he wants to get down to King John's Lakes to see what sort of junk old Josh Lovegrove keeps there.'

'Does Josh take old cars?' said the milkman. 'Because he might take this one off your hands if I don't have it.'

'Did I say anything about old cars, Ted? He only has junk.'

'That's what I mean. Scrap.'

'Listen, Ted, he don't *sell* scrap, he don't *buy* scrap, he don't even *have* scrap. Josh ain't a dealer, not in anything. He's more of a collector, that's what old Josh is, but he ain't hardly capable of knowing what he's got, or so this museum guy has told Mr Lockyer, who has a lot to do with the museum, as you know.'

'That's right,' said Ted. 'A lot.'

'You ain't taking the juice, are you, Ted, because this is serious. Mr Lockyer don't want to poke his nose in personally, but he do want to know what's happening at the Lakes. So he's asked me to keep an eye on Mr Josh Lovegrove, and be friendly to him because he's a poor old gentleman who needs help from people like me, the able-bodied.'

'You ought to be. You're getting plenty of exercise in them kitchens.'

'Never mind about that. Mr Lockyer wants me to keep an eye on things and tell him what's going on at the Lakes. And he says to me: "Take your time about it Mr

80

Bush, I'll see you won't be out of pocket".' Derek blew smoke from his nostrils. 'There's a depth of kindness in that man, Ted, that you wouldn't credit.'

'Right,' said Ted.

'But that wasn't the end of it. There was only one thing, he said, that he wouldn't have me do. He don't want me to tell anyone about it. "Mr Bush", he said, "tell me of anything we can do for the old gentleman but don't let anyone in the world know what you're doing. Because charity must be underhanded", he said, "or it ain't charity at all—self-glorification is not my way, Mr Bush." And he asked me if I'd ever seen his name in the paper for giving anything to charity, and o' course I said no, I hadn't.'

'He's a tight-arsed bugger all right,' said the milkman.

'Well, to tell you the honest truth, I might agree with you there, Ted. He don't strike me as a man who buys nuts for his bird table.'

'It takes one to know one,' said Ted. 'What's the spare like?'

'There's enough tread to get you home. What I mean is, we understood each other. He gave me what he called a watching brief to look after old Josh Lovegrove and report back to him any information I might be able to glean, are you wi' me?'

'I'm wi' you,' said the milkman.

'And then he can give Josh a bit of underhanded help if need be. Out of the goodness of his heart.'

'And he'll see you all right.'

'Well, to be quite above board with you, Ted, you couldn't expect a man in my position to trot around doing favours for people without a consideration.'

The milkman shook his head and looked out of the window. 'There's one thing I don't understand, though, Derek mate. Don't get me wrong.'

For the first time the dark eyes looked at Ted, who avoided them. 'What's that?'

81

'I'm just thinking of buying this motor off of you, right?'

'Right,' said Derek.

'And you come along and give me a lift home from work. Right?'

'Right.'

'Fair enough,' said the milkman. 'You might've just been passing.'

'I might've. So what's on your mind, Ted?'

'What I got on my mind is why are you telling me all this stuff about Mr Lockyer? Confidential stuff between you and him. That seems pretty high level information, and you'd want to keep it to yourself. To my way of thinking that is.'

'You're quite right, Ted.'

'Knowing you, you would. It needs a good clean, this motor.'

'I've got some upholstery cream, half a tin, I can let you have.'

'You wouldn't think of using it yourself, I suppose. Not like before you got rid?'

'I'm taking you into my confidence, Ted, for a very particular reason. Today is Tuesday, right?'

The milkman nodded.

'It's just a few days to go to Christmas and you'll remember that because you just got your bonus.'

'How'd you know that?'

'I'm selling my motor to you, ain't I? I got to know whether you're flush.'

For the first time the milkman's thin face creased into a smile. 'Crafty bugger,' he said. 'But my bonus won't buy no motor.'

'Maybe not, but you'll remember today and you'll remember what I was telling you today. Because what I want, to be honest wi' you, is a witness. I think that Mr Lockyer is a fine gentleman, Ted. I ain't always said so, I know, but now I see he's out to do his best for people in

82

his sneaky, underhanded, deceitful way. The world would be a far happier place if there was more like him, and I shall say so loud and clear if anybody should ask me.'

'Loud wouldn't be in it,' said the milkman.

'But I got to protect myself against him. Are you wi' me, Ted? Just in case some person should see me snooping around old Josh Lovegrove's premises and thinks it's worth his while to tell the police or anybody, I got to be able to bring out a character witness. Which is you, Ted.'

The milkman carefully dusted the ash from his cap onto the floor, while they both sat in silence. After a long pause he said, 'What she do to the gallon?'

'To be quite frank with you, there's only one fair test for a motor, and that's out on the open road. And what I do is city driving, mainly.'

'City?' said the milkman. 'Weldelph?'

'The Urban Traffic Cycle is the same the wide world over, Ted, congestion and hassle and fuming at the lights. Petrol just burns away.'

The milkman raised his eyebrows, and Derek went on hastily, 'But on a long journey I been getting thirty-five—no, I tell a lie; to be quite honest with you, thirty-three to the gallon.'

'Petrol or oil?' said the milkman.

'I'll come down fifty,' said Derek.

'Make it a ton.'

'Seventy-five.'

Their fingertips touched.

'There's nothing for you to worry about,' said Derek Bush, 'because that Mr Lockyer is genuine. He really is a *genuine* bastard, are you wi' me?'

'All the way,' said Ted and got out.

15 Cider with Charlotte

Even though she is not completely pretty, Virginia Woolf is certainly prettier than Virginia Woolf. She's not skinny for one thing, and for another her face isn't as long nor as doleful. It is, in fact, full-lipped and rounded, and she has freckles. She isn't as tall as Charlotte, who admires her a lot, particularly for her writing which is very different from Virginia Woolf's. I also enjoy the things she writes, especially as you'd expect her to keep that sort of thing secret. But you can't stop sex.

Charlotte also likes Virginia because although she's often as catty as the other Virginia she's nowhere near as Woolfish. Charlotte isn't afraid of Virginia Woolf, who's her best friend. Which is why Charlotte, just when Harry seemed to have jilted her (and the grasshopper was getting closer) told Virginia just about everything—including how she felt about Hugh Beamish at the museum and what happened when they met.

'I hope he didn't ravish you,' said Virginia, and immediately put a hand over her mouth. 'Sorry, Charlie. I mean I hope he did ravish you, or at least try. It's so demeaning if they don't.'

'I want to talk about something else,' said Charlotte, and watched Virginia screw up her face into what Virginia herself called a moue. It makes her attractive in an evil-baby kind of way. Charlotte continued, 'There's something funny going on.'

'That's predictable,' said Virginia, doing her unflappable writer bit. 'Now astonish me.'

'American Gut,' said Charlotte.

'Sounds like *True Grit*,' said Virginia. '*The Right Stuff*.'

'You're wrong by miles. It's something you can touch and feel.'

'Now we're back to handsome Hugh Beamish, the Older Man.'

Charlotte became impatient with her. 'Gin,' she said, 'you're talking in capital letters again. He's not the *Older Man*, he's just *an* older man. And I want to tell you about something else.'

'But I only asked you here, Charlie darling, so that we could exchange Girlish Confidences. You're not going to disappoint me, are you?'

'Maybe I will, maybe I won't . . .'

'. . . as the schoolgirl said to the museum curator.' Virginia poured cider from the bottle into Charlotte's glass. 'At least I've got some booze in,' she said. 'Perhaps this will loosen your tongue, as we say in Outer Mongolia.'

Virginia's Outer Mongolia is a flat in what was once a stable block behind the houses on The Sweep. Where the horses had once stamped there was now Mrs Woolf's car, and the staircase to the flat came up through the garage.

'My Mongolia is outer than yours,' said Charlotte. 'You're lucky.' Hay had once been kept in Virginia's room and there was still an uneven patch on the floor where the hay chute had been boarded over. A single circular window looked down on to a quiet road beyond which there were trees and a cricket pitch. 'No wonder you write things,' she said, 'it's just perfect here.'

'What a child you are, Charlie. You don't really think that old beams and exposed brickwork turn anybody into a writer, do you?'

'It helps.'

That's what I like about Charlotte, she's never afraid to say the obvious. She sat cross-legged on the white rug laid over the waxed floor and waved her glass at the tall bookshelves, the desk in the corner, the wooden bed with its patchwork quilt. 'Your room . . .' she sought for the words '. . . it's a ladder.' Her eyes had caught sight of the struts supporting the shelves. 'Your whole room is a ladder. Not for climbing. No, I don't mean that you're upwardly mobile or anything.'

'Thank God for that,' said Virginia.

Charlotte found herself reddening. Upwardly mobile was a Derek phrase. 'No, it's the spaces I'm talking about, not the rungs. That's what you've got. Space. And that's just what I haven't got. I've got yukky rosebud wallpaper and chests of drawers and wardrobes with things piled on top like cases and spare blankets and . . .' her mind had overreached '. . . and coat hangers.'

Virginia stared solemnly at her. 'I like "coat hangers",' she said. '"Coat hangers" is very good.'

They stared for a moment longer and then began to laugh. Virginia was propped against a bean bag. 'Charlie,' she said, 'you're drunk.' She patted the cushion at her side. 'Lay your head here and tell me about American Gut.'

Charlotte stretched herself out. 'And another thing you've got,' she said, 'is a radiator. My room's freezing.'

'You don't have to be sorry for yourself, Charlie, not with your looks. What *is* American Gut?'

'There's nothing wrong with the way you look either, Gin.'

'Capital M, capital A, capital S. Mutual Admiration Society. I've got a smudge for a face.'

'Well, I'll tell you something now. I heard that new boy say you were like Cider with Rosie and he'd love to squash up close to you.'

Which was quite true. I had said it.

'Is he the one who thinks he's a writer?' said Virginia.

'Yes.'

'You see what I mean,' Virginia sighed, 'it's merely literary. He wants to hold hands with Virginia Woolf or Mrs Dalloway, the pervert.'

'Whatever it is, he fancies you.'

Which I did—and still do in spite of what Virginia, as one writer to another, told me happened that afternoon.

'And the trouble is I *am* like Mrs Dalloway,' said Virginia, 'I must be liked, I talk oceans of nonsense, and to this day if you ask me where the Equator is I don't know.'

'End quote,' said Charlotte, who had heard this before.

'But I do know his sort, Charlie. He wants me to write him into one of my porny stories, and I wouldn't go anywhere near anybody who wanted *that*.'

'Everyone wants to be in that sort of story, Gin.'

'Even you? Beautiful you? And all those horrible men I dream up—I can't bear to think of it. What *is* American Gut?'

Charlotte closed her eyes. Her skirt lay loosely over her legs and the neck of her blouse was open but, in this house, she was warm. 'I think it's some sort of string and I expect old Josh Lovegrove needs it for something pretty peculiar.'

'Like his walking stick.'

Charlotte, refusing to laugh, was aware that Virginia was stroking her hair where it was spread over the cushion. 'Whatever it is, it's something he's got hidden away down at the Lakes. Harry said he was going to try to get him some from his father's warehouse.'

She paused, thinking, while Virginia stroked her hair. Suddenly her eyes opened wide. 'I've been a traitor, Gin! Harry didn't want me to spread it around, but I did.' She raised herself on one elbow so swiftly that her hair, caught between Virginia's fingers, jerked her head back.

It was a punishment she deserved. 'Harry Green didn't want me to tell anybody, but I did. I told Hugh Beamish, and now I'm telling you.'

'Why?'

'I told you.' Charlotte's head was stretched back and her voice was strangled. 'Because Harry let that man say things about me in his father's office.'

'I don't blame you, Charlie.' But Virginia was distracted by the curve of Charlotte's throat. 'You have a neck like a . . . like a . . .'

'Swan?'

'Swan is a cliché, Charlie. Your neck is as smooth as a barley stem bent by the wind, and your chin is as white as . . .'

'A swan?'

'As a duck's bottom. Did he kiss it?'

'Who'd want to kiss my chin?'

'Your curator.'

'You want to know too much.'

'Yes, I do, Charlie darling. I always want to know everything. You told me that man in the warehouse said nasty things about you, but you didn't tell me what. Something terrible, I hope.'

Charlotte lowered her eyes. 'Well, it wasn't about me personally. It was Derek.'

'Oh, Charlie, you have all the advantages!' They were resting on their elbows now, face to face. 'I don't begrudge you your looks, but I do envy you your brother who's been in prison. There's me who really *needs* to know what it's like to do porridge and I've never even seen the outside of a nick, never mind getting inside a cell like you.'

'I haven't been in a cell either.'

'But you went to see him in chokey. You've heard the prison gates clang shut behind you.'

'They don't clang, they thud.'

'That's just what I mean. You *know* and I only *guess*.

Still,' she sighed, 'people don't get hanged in prisons any more, no glamour left.'

'Some doors clang. And you're always hearing keys jangle. All the warders have big bunches of keys dangling from their belts.'

'Screws, darling. They have the keys for when they bang the prisoners up for the night. And then there's all those peepholes set in little round hollows in the doors. I always think they're bra-shaped. Wouldn't it be a lovely cool iron feel?'

'There's some patches of lawn outside,' said Charlotte, 'and the paths are very neat.' As horribly neat as thin hair, scratched and raked to perfection. 'And the place we met him was a sort of hut in the yard.' It was like a tea room in a park; tables and chairs spaced out. 'Scrubbed clean,' she said.

'Did you and your mother take him some snout? He does smoke, doesn't he, your brother Derek?'

'He cried,' said Charlotte. 'He said he wanted to kill himself.'

'Did he!' Virginia was gazing eagerly into her face. 'Wasn't that thoughtful of him! He'd brought shame on his family and didn't want to embarrass them any longer.'

'You don't understand anything, Ginny.'

'Gin, if you please. I don't want to be mistaken for a tedious tennis person. I think your Derek is heroic. Seedy-looking, but absolutely the Right Stuff, wanting to die for others.'

'I couldn't have cared if he did.'

'Charlotte!'

'Nor could his wife. She never went to see him, not once, and I don't blame her.'

'Char-*lotte*, your hatred of your brother is terrifying!' Virginia's eyes were gleaming. 'You're a vicious little cat, a murderess. No wonder that curator has the hots for you.'

'You might think differently about my brother if you knew him as intimately as I do.'

'Intimately!' Virginia drew in her breath. 'Not with his own little sister!'

'You want a bit too much, Virginia.'

'But I have so little, Charlie. I'm deprived. You've got a criminal brother, but I haven't even got a father around the house, at least not often. Just supposing wicked Derek and you . . . it would make an absolutely wrenching story.'

'He's been questioning me, Gin. All of a sudden he wants to know what I know about Josh Lovegrove and the Lakes.'

'And American Gut, I suppose.'

'Well, he would, if I ever mentioned it. He even knows I've been to the museum and he asks me questions about it. He wants to know about everything.'

'So do I. I want to know all about the exquisite Hugh, your beamish boy.'

'I'm worried, Gin.'

Virginia's voice took on a serious tone, as though she had a book and was reading. '*As Charlotte sat in the flickering firelight in his office, his tall figure got to its feet and, moving with the silence of thought, he came to stand beside her chair.*'

Charlotte gave a little snort. 'How do you know?'

'*He stooped over and she raised her face so that, for one wicked second, the firelight gave her eyes such a golden, murderous glow he was terrified.*'

'Shut up, Gin. I'm worried in case Derek has got something in his mind.'

'*Terror was in Hugh Beamish's mind. Who was this golden girl who drew him closer and closer?*' As she spoke, Virginia Woolf came further and further forward until her breath stirred Charlotte's hair. '*Her skin was as palely glowing as the promise of her thighs.*'

90

'Her thighs promised nothing. I refuse to be in one of your stories, Gin.'

'You already are. My words are touching you with the same insane delicacy that made you tremble as his lips brushed your cheek.'

'But what if Derek is planning something? He keeps asking about Hugh Beamish—he might want to steal something from the museum!'

Charlotte lifted her hand, but as she did so Virginia spaced her words to fit the action. *'Charlotte raised her hand, intending to push him from her, but he reached across her and their fingers met and intertwined.'* Virginia herself reached and clasped Charlotte's hand.

'You're bending my fingers, Gin. You're hurting.'

'"You're hurting me!" she cried. But the fullness of her parted lips was too much for him and he stooped towards her.'

'Gin! Go away!'

'Her cry was smothered as their spittle mingled.'

16 American Gut

Harry loves machinery, which is why what eventually happened was such a bitter blow for him. He also has a real problem with his father. So have I with mine, but we're not in absolute competition all the time, although my mother reckons we are. The trouble with my old man is that sometimes he tries too hard to be a 'good parent', and then I have to introduce a bit of anarchy to rattle him out of it. This would never work with Harry's father; all he wants to do is stamp you down, Harry included. Which means that Harry, even though he enjoys going to his father's warehouse, would never admit it.

So Harry had mixed feelings when he went to the warehouse with his father to load up the American Gut for old Josh. I know exactly the faraway expression on Harry's face as he watched the hoist lift the two coils of gut clear of the warehouse floor. The chains of the hoist, silvered smooth by generations of use, slid like silk over the pulleys and soothed his mind in the way machinery always did.

'Enough there to keep old Josh happy, d'you reckon?' said Julian Green. The coils, each sewn into covers of burlap, were the size of small barrels.

'He's not expecting to get them for nothing, Dad.'

'They're no good to me, Harry boy. Didn't even know we had 'em.'

'He'd like to pay something.'

Harry did not even expect a reply, and did not listen for one. Instead, he gave himself up to the pleasure of hearing the chiming rattle of the hoist's ratchet, and seeing it lock and hold the two heavy coils at waist height. The warehouse was like a windmill with its moving parts big enough to walk among and see how they connected. There were flaps in the floor. Ever since he could remember he had enjoyed watching bales and heavy sacks hauled upwards towards a solid ceiling which, at the moment of contact, split open as the bales nudged the flaps aside to sail through into the space beyond. Then the flaps slapped down and the ceiling was solid again. Some time, somewhere, a genius had invented the split flap.

His father always noticed the difference in his son whenever they were in the warehouse and it put him in a good humour. The warehouse was about the only place where they understood each other.

'You and old Josh was lucky to find that stuff, Harry,' he said. 'Lucky it's still in good nick and the rats ain't got it. Any idea what he wants it for?'

'No.'

'Funny stuff.' They had opened one coil and pulled out a length of the gut. It was a dull white, as thick as a finger and knobbed in places like knuckles. 'They used it because it stretched, did you know that? Not like rubber, which wasn't much good in them days anyway, but when they wanted something with just a bit of spring in it. The Red Indians used to make it out of buffalo intestines. That's where it came from, the real stuff, American buffaloes. I should think that was paid for in silver dollars; either that or whisky.'

'How do you know all this?' Harry stood alongside his father, sensing the friendliness that came as quick as his anger.

'It's not only that fairy at the museum that can do a bit of research.' His father grinned, and Harry smiled back at him. 'I've got a trade handbook in my desk that belonged to my great grandfather, and it's all there. Seems it was highly thought of for really delicate springing jobs like some sorts o' light carriages instead of them iron leaf springs, and the stuff could be stretched round a drum to keep bits of machinery going.'

'Like roasting spits, you mean?'

'That sort o' thing. And rocking babies' cradles. Old Josh Lovegrove ain't got a baby hid away down at them Lakes, has he?'

Harry laughed with him.

Two of his father's men were working the hoist, and now they had stopped to raise the flaps and lower the coils to the next floor.

'Talkin' of museums,' said his father, 'this is just like working in one, ain't it? I'd have had a proper electric hoist to do that if them buggers on the council had let me put one in.' He spoke loud enough for the two men to overhear him. They were both young, hardly older than Harry. 'Automation,' he said, 'then you two wouldn't have had no job at all.'

'Up,' said one, whose long hair hid his face. His mate

went to the chains and raised the coils which were jamming the flaps. 'Steady.'

'Steady it is, my son,' said Julian Green. 'Steady old job is what you've got to be thankful for in this day and age.'

'Shit!' said the boy as the heavy coils swung and jammed his hand against the guard rail.

Harry stepped in front of his father and heaved at one of the ropes of the sling but succeeded only in making the load turn so that the boy had to force it the other way to free his hand. 'You all right?' said Harry.

The boy had a bony white brow and a fuzz of hair on his lip. He had a very small mouth which stayed shut.

'Sorry,' said Harry.

The boy nodded to his mate, who had made no effort to help but stood by the chains, bare-armed in a sleeveless leather jerkin. He hauled, and the pair of them, working together, swung the load clear of the flaps.

His father abruptly turned away and went downstairs, leaving Harry to smile apologetically at the two boys for not having helped more effectively. They ignored him.

The Volvo, with its tailgate up, had been backed up to the loading quay. 'We ain't got all morning,' said his father. 'Get in.'

'I'll help them load.'

'In!' His father got into the driver's seat and slammed the door.

Harry obeyed, aware of his father's hands clenching and unclenching on the steering wheel. Then it came.

'Never do that again.' His father gazed directly ahead as though he was already driving.

'Never do what?'

'Prat about trying to do their work for them.'

'I was only trying to help. He could have been hurt.'

'I don't give a damn if he broke his bloody arm.' His

94

father kept his voice low, with an effort, but he was pounding the rim of the wheel with the heel of his palm. 'You made a fool of yourself up there.' His mouth shut and he drew in a deep breath through his nose. 'And you made a fool of me as well. Never again.'

Harry's mouth was dry. 'I was only trying to help.'

His father's head came round slowly, everything under control. 'Trying to help, were you? What do you think I pay them for? So that I can have the privilege of *helping* them? Let me tell you, my son, that pair up there are bloody lucky to have any sort of job at all.'

'So you kept telling them, my father.'

The paw that slid down the steering wheel was ready to lash out. Instead, it gripped, holding itself in check. 'What's this "my father" crap? Did you know you nearly got a back-hander then?'

'I did.' Harry pushed his face forward. When he does that he looks like a sort of blond pug dog. 'Yes, I did. My father.'

The hand left the wheel, drawn back in one swift motion, but for the first time in his life Harry's eyes did not leave his father's. He longed to be hit. He yearned for it so that his hatred would blaze to a peak that nothing, for the rest of time, would quench. He even began to smile at the glory of it as his father's hand dropped back to the wheel.

'By Christ, Harry boy, you'll never know how near you came to it then.'

'You've hit me before.'

'Not since you was a little kid.'

'You've hit me.'

'"You've hit me, Daddy." Stop talking like a jessy and act your bloody age. Of course I've bloody well hit you, and I'll hit those two yobs back there if they don't get their fingers out.' He hunched himself around to watch the two youths rolling the coils across the loading quay. He swung back suddenly. 'What you don't understand,

95

Harry, is that they got their pride just the same as you. They don't want your help. You're the boss's son. They were telling you to sod off, up there, that's what they were doing.'

'And you.'

'Of course they bloody were. I was needling them, wasn't I? Going on about how lucky they was to have jobs. Because I'm the boss and they expect it. So they get back at me don't they, with dumb bloody insolence? *They* know it, *I* know it. Why did you think that one with the bare arms was showing off his tattoos? Because all the time I could see his muscles he was saying, "Up you, Guv—and up your bloody son, an' all."'

'Very good industrial relations, that is.'

'Industrial bloody relations my arse. Let me tell you, my son . . .' His finger was beginning to wag, but he saw more trouble in Harry's eye. 'Oh, what's the bloody use!' and he rolled down the window to shout, 'Get your skates on, I got a customer waiting.'

The tailgate banged shut and a slap on the roof set them rolling up the narrow back street towards the river. 'You don't know what I'm about, do you, Harry? I'm a puzzle to you, right?'

His father's eyes looked sideways at him, but Harry said nothing, made no move. He told me there was a lot he wanted to say but he didn't have the nerve.

'You think I'm just a hard old sod,' said his father. No response from Harry. The knuckles whitened. 'You're giving me a hard time, son.'

Yes, Father. I'm glad, Father. That's what was in Harry's mind, but his mouth stayed closed.

They crossed the bridge and turned right, heading upstream. Neither spoke, and soon the curve of the river and the high floodbank put the town out of sight. The frosty fenland spread out in front of their windscreen.

'You'll have to tell me if I can drive right up to Josh's place, I ain't that sure.'

'There's a track.'

A meagre snow had dusted land that was so flat and hard that at every shift of the iron air the reeds sieved the restless grains to send up wisps of white smoke. Harry did not have to get out to allow his father to drive into Josh's domain, for the wooden gate in the hedge stood open.

'What a dump.' His father eased the Volvo through the gap. 'I'd be happier if this was a marsh buggy.' The car, its wheel arches bearded with ice, rocked and slithered in the track that wound between the clumps of bushes that edged the frozen water. Manhandling the car through this was something they both enjoyed, and Harry relented.

'I should think the ice is thick enough to drive over,' he said.

His father spun the wheels, slewing the rear end and picking up traction as they turned another sharp bend. 'King John's Lakes!' he said. 'More like bloody ponds. But they go on for ever. When do we get there?'

'In a minute.' Harry had little idea and did not want to admit that the last time he had actually been to the Lakes was when he was a kid. He had tried to swim there but the mud was too deep and he had fled at the sight of old Josh. 'It's different in winter,' he said.

'He don't allow fishing, I believe, or else I'd have tried. More fool him. He could charge.'

'He likes his privacy.'

'Privacy is what you have if you've got the cash, and that is what Joshua Lovegrove don't have much of. Just look at that if you don't believe me.' An old punt, half rotted, was frozen to the bank, its stern under the ice. 'What a dump.'

But suddenly they came through a gap in the brambles and tall bushes and were in an open space. Directly opposite them, as though it had just pulled into a station on some secret branch line, stood a railway carriage. It

97

was partly screened by a low hedge, which gave the impression that the locomotive was just out of sight.

'Well, bugger me!' said Julian Green. 'I know he said so, but I never believed that people still lived in them things.'

The carriage doors still had traces of large yellow numerals, first and third class, but its wheels had gone and the carriage rested on heavy baulks of timber. There was even, along part of its length, a little veranda.

'You'd never credit it,' said his father, but Harry hardly heard him. He had vaguely wondered, as they came into Josh's territory, why the gate was open, but now he knew. At the edge of the open space, away to the left, another car was parked and somebody had paused just before getting into it to drive off.

Harry's father wound his window down as the driver of the other car came towards them.

'I'm afraid you're out of luck if you wish to see the old gentleman,' said Hugh Beamish. 'He doesn't seem to be at home.'

But Harry was looking beyond him to his passenger. Charlotte sat in Beamish's old blue mini. She was combing her hair.

17 The Watchers

It was a bitter night and the Cortina coughed quietly as it rolled into the layby, cut its engine, and shut its eyes.

'Dark,' said the milkman. 'It's going to be cold up there with no heating on.' The layby was on the flood-bank that made a thick wall across the fens. 'You put anti-freeze in it?'

'That radiator has got so much anti-freeze it's glutted

with it, stuffed with it, full to the bloody gills with so much bloody anti-freeze it's practically running over.'

'That's what I thought,' said the milkman. 'There's always a pool underneath.'

'All cars drip, Ted. Brand-new cars *drip*.'

'It must be very cold tonight,' said Ted, 'because that anti-freeze is making little icicles underneath.'

'You've only got to look at that river out there to see how *exceptionally* cold it is. There's ice-floes coming up with the tide, and that's mostly sea-water, Ted, practically pure salt.'

'Like your anti-freeze.'

'Which has been in all summer, so it's full of residual heat like the ocean.'

'That's a comfort,' said the milkman.

Derek Bush, in the passenger seat, rubbed the window and gazed away from the river across the flat fenland. It was burnished both by moonlight and the icy wind. 'You heard what he said, Ted? You heard Mr Lockyer's actual words?'

'Couldn't hardly help it,' said the milkman, 'not with you pushing the phone in my ear.'

'I had to make sure.'

'There wasn't no need for it though. With us squashed together in that box, I could hear him quite clear anyway.'

'I needed a witness. I got to protect myself.'

'It was me needed protection. You carry quite a bit of weight, Derek mate, and there weren't much room in there.'

'I'm working it off.'

'It was like having a third person in that box. You and me and it.'

'All *right*, Ted. I'm getting rid of it.'

'Because I tell you what, you was leaning against me and it was me who was bearing the weight of it. Did you realize you was resting on me? I don't suppose you did

99

because it's so far away from you I expect it's difficult for you to keep in touch.'.

'Listen, Ted, listen.'

'I doubt you ever noticed. I suppose something big and thick-skinned like an elephant can come along and lean on a person in quite a friendly way and flatten you out o' recognition and then look round and be quite surprised at what it done. I mean I think I come out of that phone box with quite a curve. I was sort of bent over, did you notice?'

'Ted!'

'I'm not calling you an elephant or anything like that, Derek. Don't get me wrong.'

'That's all right, Ted.'

'It's just that you've got a big gut on you.'

'Ted! Did you hear what he said, Ted? The words he actually spoke, whispered, yelled, dictated, uttered, *micturated* down that telephone?'

'I did.'

'Well?'

'What he said,' said Ted, 'was "Well done, Bush, thank you". And then you was oiling round him.'

'Thank you for what? What was it he thanked me for?'

'For your report. That's what he said.'

'For my report. You got to remember that's what he said, Ted. And then what?'

'And then he hoped you'd keep your eyes open and keep in touch. And then you was greasing him up again, saying you certainly would, Mr Lockyer sir.'

'You got it now, Ted. You heard him encouraging me to spy and snoop around them Lakes after I told him I seen what I seen—which was Mr Julian Green *and* that young feller from the museum doing their own bit o' snooping because they think old Josh has got something valuable. Right?'

'Right,' said Ted.

100

'Which proves he's commissioned me to act as his undercover agent. Which is what I am.'

'Which is why we're up here freezing to death in the middle of the night,' said the milkman. 'In my car.'

'Ted.' Derek Bush turned away from the window to face him. 'I'm helping you to run it in.'

'I thought we was testing it to destruction.'

'Ted.'

'I reckon we've just about managed it.'

'Listen, Ted, listen. Running it in is just something we say if anybody wants to know why we're parked up here in the middle of the night.'

'Running it in by standing still. That'll keep us in the clear all right.'

'Either that or you are familiarizing yourself with the control system. I got to have a cover story, Ted, and you got to get to know your new car, ain't you?'

'That's right. Where's the owner's handbook?'

'Handbook? Have you ever noticed that handbooks always tell you about things you haven't got on that particular model?'

'I know,' said the milkman, 'and what this particular model ain't got is a handbook.'

'I'll get you one.'

'It don't matter because I wouldn't be able to read it. The roof light don't work.'

'There's nothing wrong with the courtesy light, Ted. I took out the bulb because you don't want that coming on to show everybody who you are every time you open the door. You want a bit of privacy now and again.'

''Course you do,' said the milkman. 'Especially for your kind o' work. Undercover.'

'I've got him under surveillance now.' Derek Bush was looking out of the window. 'There's still a light on in the old railway carriage. I wonder what he's doing.'

'There's one thing he can't be doing.'

'What's that?'

'Having a pee. You can't do that while the train's in the station.'

'Which reminds me.' Derek opened the door. 'I got to go.'

'Watch you don't get it frozen to the bushes,' said the milkman.

18 The Christmas Tree

When I first met Harry, that day in the common room, I was quite rude to him but I insulted him out of sympathy. Charlotte was too good-looking for him, and I know what it feels like to be out of your depth, so I butted in. Real beauty is just too much to live up to.

He could have bopped me; instead, he began to tell me things, and in the end I was acting as a sort of go-between for both of them. They told me things they couldn't quite bring themselves to say to each other. It was like being drawn into a whirlpool, because once it started it spun faster and faster until they were letting me into secrets they never told anybody else.

There was the day of the Christmas tree, for instance. I found out all about that from Harry himself. The tree was in his house and he was helping his mother to decorate it a few hours after he and his father had taken the American Gut to Josh Lovegrove's railway carriage.

'We didn't see him,' said Julian Green, 'so we left the stuff in his porch.'

'Poor old man.' Roz Green had draped tinsel over the large tree in the front window and was hanging baubles among the branches. 'Sounds horrible,' she said, 'American Gut. What can he want stuff like that for?'

'We ain't the only ones that don't know. Right, Harry boy?'

102

Harry grunted. He wanted to change the subject but was too slow. He should have gone out, anywhere rather than be here doing this. She always wanted everything to be perfect for Christmas. Cosy. Now she said, 'Answer your Dad, Harry. Be nice.'

'I am nice. I've got nothing to say, that's all.'

'Leave him be, Roz.' His father was at his ease, sprawled in a deep armchair half way along the length of the long room. 'He's had his nose put out of joint, that's all.'

'How do you mean?' Harry turned his back on the tree to face him. 'I don't know what you mean.'

'You wasn't too pleased to see that fairy from the museum with your bird.'

'She's not my *bird*! She's not a bird at all.'

'Who are we talking about?' Roz tried to keep the peace. I've seen the way she would have cocked her head and looked roguishly at her son. 'Which young lady are we talking about, may I ask?'

If they had been alone Harry would have told her, but he shrugged and his father answered for him. 'You'd know her if you saw her. You got to admire his taste, Roz. I wouldn't blame any bloke for chasin' that, in spite of everything.'

'Don't let him tease you.' Roz felt sorry for her son. 'She still at school?'

'If you can call it that,' said his father. 'She ain't got no need of school, that one. And she knows it.'

'He's crude, your father. He don't mean it like it sounds. What's her name?'

Harry told her Charlotte's name, and shifted his eyes to his father. He raised his voice. 'She lives in a lousy little house along the Drove and her brother goes to prison because he steals.'

'I never said a word,' said Julian Green.

'But you would have done.' Harry looked at his mother. Exasperation tightened the muscles of his face

103

and made his eyes sting. 'She's got no father,' he said. 'He's dead.'

'Oh, Harry.' Roz had tears in her eyes. 'But she's nice, is she, Harry?'

He nodded, not able to speak.

'I tell you what, Roz.' It was impossible to tell from his father's voice if he realized what was happening. 'There wasn't talent like that around in my day.'

'Hark at him,' she said to Harry and then turned to her husband. 'Thank you very much for the compliment, Julian Green. You always did know how to make a girl feel good.'

'I had the charm, didn't I? And the money.'

'I don't know what happened to the charm,' she said, 'and I never did see much of the money.'

I've been in Harry's house when they've been going on at each other like this and I've enjoyed it because they include you. It's just like being in the common room, but this time Harry had had enough. He glanced away through the window. 'More snow,' he said.

'Snow!' His father was disgusted. 'That's all we bloody need.'

'I like it,' said Roz. 'It's Christmassy.'

Harry heard the traditional sentimental whine in her voice. The endlessly drawn out vowel of li-i-i-ike and the dying fall of Christmas-ee, and he knocked a bauble from its branch.

'Harree!' she cried.

'It didn't break.' The carpet was too thick to let it smash. He considered putting his foot on it.

'Give it here,' she said. 'You're as clumsy as your father.' She hooked it among the pine needles. 'Oh I do feel sorry for people who haven't got the money to enjoy theirselves at Christmas.'

'Never mind about the starving millions,' said her husband. 'This snow keeps up and we'll be among 'em.'

'Scrooge, that's what you are.'

'You want to look at my books for this month, that's all. We're not shifting a thing, not a bloody thing, and now it's bloody snowing.'

Harry said, 'I like Scrooge. He's mean and selfish and cruel—the real spirit of Christmas.'

'You're coming to your senses at last,' said his father. 'I never thought you would.'

'And I like a tree,' said Roz Green, 'it's worth all the mess. Anyway you can soon Hoover up the needles.' She faced Harry. 'What you so glum about? Scrooge is only a story, you know.'

'What we ought to get for this tree,' he said, 'is a reindeer with a red nose that lights up.'

'They got them in Woolworths,' she said. 'I nearly bought one.'

Harry allowed himself to sink to the floor, pretending he was inspecting the flex to the lights. He crawled behind the tub, hiding the wires at the edges of the bay window in which the tree stood, a Christmas sentinel. It was like being a kid again, making Christmas caves.

'You can switch on when you like,' he said, but he remained where he was, kneeling by the window and looking out. It was getting dark, and the winter garden was being sheeted down under a white tarpaulin. In the silent road a car nosed through the falling snow and drew a turmoil of snowflakes behind it like a fluttering skirt that hid its rear. The night was white and black outside, but then the glass in front of him was suddenly crusted with darts and stabs of coloured light.

'Ooh!' cried Roz. 'Fairyland!'

Harry saw his own silhouette against the bright pyramid of the tree in the glass but he did not turn round.

'I wish it was always Christmas,' she said. 'I never get tired of it.' Harry heard his father grunt, and then she said, 'Oh, come on, Julian, it's nowhere near as bad businesswise as you make out. I know you've got something up your sleeve.'

'What if I haven't? What if I go bust?'

'Just listen to yourself.' She was laughing at him. 'You sit there with your fat old cheeks all droopy and gloomy instead of rosy like they should be, and you've got pots of money, you know you have. Come on, Santa Claus, give us a smile.'

Harry heard a scuffle and his mother squealed, 'Take your hands off me, you wolf!'

'I want my Christmas present.'

'Later. Not here, you horrible man.'

'I want it now.'

'I'll call my son. He'll protect me.'

He could hear her giggling and gasping as she struggled to free herself. Once he would have charged in and been moiled about among their arms and legs, rolled over and over and pummelled like dough until laughter and exhaustion left them in a heap.

'Harry!' she cried.

'What?'

'Help!'

It was then, quite suddenly, he realized, ridiculously, he no longer had the fat little arms she had loved to squeeze.

'Harry! Help!'

He remained where he was and the scuffles became quieter and then ceased. 'Lot o' good you were, Harry,' she called. 'I've lost a button off me shirt and me hair's in a mess.' She squealed again. 'Get off, you pig! If you ain't got no money I don't want any more to do with you.'

Julian Green laughed. 'We're going to be all right, Rozzie. I have got something up my sleeve, genuine.'

'It ain't much good up there,' and both of them laughed while their son shut his eyes.

After a while Roz said, 'I might've known you was up

106

to something. You got that look on your face like a cat that's had the cream. And I know something else an' all—it's something to do with King John's Lakes.'

'Harry told you.'

'No, he didn't. I worked it out myself. It just ain't like you, Julian Green, to give anything away without wanting something in return, so when you told me you was giving that American stuff to that old man Lovegrove I guessed you must be up to something. I ain't just a pretty face.'

'I'm going to buy his land.'

When he told me this, Harry's expression did not change. He'd known all along that his father wanted to buy the land, but he had never asked why. The truth was that he was afraid to find out. If his father wasn't being fair to old Josh, Harry didn't want to know. But now it was out in open he could not prevent himself listening. The news was a big surprise to his mother.

'Buy King John's Lakes?' she said. 'What on earth you want to do that for?'

'I'm not at liberty to divulge at this stage.' His father was teasing her, enjoying himself. And he knew Harry was listening. 'But I can tell you, just in case my son and heir is getting worried behind that tree over there, that old Josh Lovegrove ain't going to be done out of anything. He's going to be offered a fair price—very fair, considering what it is I'm buying.'

'So it's not settled?' said Roz.

'Not quite, but it will be. Why d'you think I been spending so much time with Lockyer? We got a deal.'

Harry listened for her reaction. She was bound to be pleased. She would squeal and say her husband was clever. But the room behind his back was silent. She must be kissing him. After a moment he realized the pause was caused by something else. His mother had doubts.

'I don't like that man, Julian,' she said.

107

'I thought it was Lady Lockyer you didn't go for.'

'Her an' all, but she's just stuck up and stupid. It's him I can't abide. He's too smooth for me.'

'Don't get me riled, Roz. I'm in partnership with him, and he's a bloody good business man.'

'I wouldn't trust him as far as I could throw him. He's got all-seeing eyes.'

The silence could have been anger, but Julian Green suddenly burst into laughter. 'All-seeing eyes! I like that one, Rozzie—all-seeing eyes is good. What d'you think my eyes are like?'

'Pissholes in the snow,' she said, and the scuffle started again.

'But I don't trust him, Roz. O' course I bloody don't. What do you think I went down the Lakes for, when I don't need to? It ain't just the land I'm interested in. Because that museum feller wasn't down there just for nothing. He was on the look-out for antiques, that's what he was doin'. And if old Josh has got somethin' among his junk that's worth a bit I don't want it whipped out from under my nose.'

Harry came out from hiding. 'I can tell you what he's got,' he said.

His mother and father both lay on the floor. She had one hand under her head and one leg in its tight jeans was bent in the pose of a model girl. 'What's he got then, Harry?' she said.

'A bull's pizzle.'

He went out, leaving them laughing.

19 The Grasshopper

Joshua Lovegrove is a small man so it was very easy for him, crouching slightly, to pass beneath the belly of the grasshopper. Then he straightened and reached up to one of the green segments of its body just a little way back from its armour-plated head. He turned a catch, and the curved section hinged upwards. The grasshopper trembled along its length, and its reddish eyes, the size of coconuts, caught a gleam of light in their internal facets and glimmered briefly.

'Steady,' he murmured. 'Steady.'

He hooked up the side plate so that it remained open and looked inside. This was the heart chamber, there could be no doubt about that. Everything was ultimately connected here, except that for generations no connections had been made. There were many gaps.

He took a pace towards the rear of the creature and lifted another of its body plates where the green sheen shaded to yellow. The hollow cavity was criss-crossed by rods that, judging by their joints and pivots, were intended for movement, although now they were motionless.

'And no wheels,' he said. 'Has anybody noticed that? No wheels!' He raised his voice and turned as though he was asking a genuine question and was in the presence of an audience who would answer, but the wide floor of his barn was empty, swept clean.

It was dusk, but the sacking curtains at the windows had been neatly hooked back so that the snowlight from outside filled the space from rafters to floor with a paleness that cast no shadow. He went on with his inspection, still lecturing.

'The weakness of the wheel,' he said, 'is that it has to be a separate part. It has to move independently, it cannot be joined to what it carries—and, without a joint, it can form no part of a living creatuar. How do you join a wheel to an elephant? Where are the wheels of a giraffe? Could an antelope bound over bushes on wheels? And pray consider the centipede—the humble centiwheel.'

109

The idea amused him, forcing him to celebrate with a jig, his feet disappearing under the long skirts of his coat.

'There is no wheel in natuar. Natuar abhors the wheel. Go oil me an elephant's axle!'

Eyes were watching him. A figure had crept up to the barn and was peering through a window beneath a swathe of the sacking curtain. It saw a grinning dwarf in a bobble hat swinging a whippy cane.

'On the other hand,' said Josh, 'a pendulum has nothing to do but fall.' He kicked up a foot. 'A leg is a pendulum, and so is an arm. They swing beneath an elephant, and they propel the stately giraffe.' He chanted: 'My Uncle Cox he knew it all, a pendulum does naught but fall.' And with the tip of his cane he described in the air a downward swinging arc. 'Down, down, down and then up, up, up—but still falling. Oh my uncle, my genius!'

He swung around so quickly that the eyes, believing they had been spotted, ducked beneath the sill just as he touched with the tip of his cane the inner workings of the grasshopper.

When the watcher raised his head again, the grasshopper's flat-fronted head was nodding. The dwarf, a shadow now in the failing light, nodded back.

PART FOUR

20 Finger on the Pulse

I was beginning to see that the private whirlpool of Harry and Charlotte was itself being drawn into deeper currents. At the centre, but still so deep that only a few secret eyes had yet caught a glimpse of it, was the grasshopper. I'm going to tell my father about the grasshopper some day, but not yet—because I'm not sure how he'll react to what Charlotte did in the end. Fathers who are also teachers are a dodgy bet in some respects—inclined to be moralistic about what girls get up to. If I do tell him, I'll let Mum soften him up first. She'd understand why Charlotte did what she did.

But Dad has his uses. For instance he was quite friendly with the person who was really responsible for bringing the Weldelph Scandal into the open. Not Robin Horn. Dad didn't work it out until later, but the funny thing is it was all quite plain to anybody who went to that little bar under the stairs and kept his ears open. Which my father did, especially that day very close to Christmas.

He'd gone out for a pint with a bunch of other staff-room boozers, which was why he didn't join Robin Horn at the next table with Hugh Beamish, but he overheard him say, 'How's about that for a picture of a bored barman?'

'Awe-inspiring,' said Hugh Beamish, and both of them gazed at George behind the bar.

'But note his finger,' said Robin. Even from his place in the corner my father could see that, where George's large hands were spread on the bar, a single finger

111

pulsed like a tethered caterpillar. 'Proof that there's life after death,' said Robin. 'He's not missing a thing. That finger, old boy, is on the pulse of Weldelph.'

Hugh Beamish became sly. 'He must be a useful man for a newspaperman to know,' he said, but Robin didn't rise to it. He seemed in a gloomy frame of mind. Hugh went on, 'George is so much of a character I wonder the *Messenger* doesn't do a story on him.'

'Maybe we will. Who can tell?'

'Perhaps I'll suggest it to Mr Puckeridge.'

That made Robin look up sharply. 'Over my dead body, old boy.'

'At least I've brought you to life. Why so pensive and so woebegone?'

'Thoughts too black for a human mind to bear.' Robin picked up his lighter from the pile of change in front of him and lit a cigarette. 'I look at old George over there staring into nothingness and I see the bleak side of Christmas. It's a black hole, Hugh, and it opens at our feet. It is covered over with tinsel but it swallows us all.' He dragged on his cigarette.

'And the sight of George brought this on?'

'It's the blackness in the bush, old boy. The heart of the Christmas tree is dark.'

The barman's red face above the tight collar and tie was immobile. My father, as he told my mother later, suddenly realized that somewhere, in the back alleyways of the market place, there was a cold little flat where George would go when the bar lights were switched off.

Hugh Beamish said, 'Well, if it's not George who's making you so gloomy, what is it? Don't you have anywhere to go at Christmas, Robin?'

'Me?' Robin was surprised. 'There's a small hotel in a distant shire where I roast a chestnut or two at yuletide. Don't worry about me, old son, anywhere upwind of the Puke suffices.'

'Then it *is* George. You're sorry for him.'

'You don't want to worry about him, either. He's an old salt sailor, is George, come aground on a lee shore. He could exist on the juice of an oilskin button. But cast your eye at that bar and tell me what you see.'

Two customers sat on bar stools with their backs to the room. At that time my father did not know who they were, but it was fairly obvious that Hugh did from the nervous way he lowered his voice. Nevertheless he played along with Robin. 'What I see,' he said, 'is two self-satisfied backsides.'

'Weldelph's best,' said Robin. 'Part of the Con Club clique, keep the rates down and save our grammar school.'

My father was delighted. Private schooling sends him berserk. From now on he was Robin's man, and listening hard. Hugh Beamish seemed to be on the right side as well.

'There's quite a few of them around,' he said. 'Big cars with ignorance at the wheel.'

'The cream of the cream, Hugh, and you're gazing upon their thinking ends, where the words come from.'

And then Hugh put two and two together. Once again he looked across the room at George standing motionless behind the bar. 'The finger on the pulse,' he said. 'That's how you find out what's going on. George listens.'

'And hates 'em.' Robin raised his voice. 'Isn't that so, George—you've got no time for any of 'em?' He grimaced at the two backs just before the heads turned his way.

'Very little, sir.'

George winked. It had all become so open that my father was sure Hugh Beamish had gone pale, especially when one of the men appeared to recognize him. And Robin seemed determined to make it worse. He got to his feet and went up to the bar. 'George hasn't got time for a man who won't take a drink at Christmas,' he said.

113

'Quite so, Mr Horn.'

'Same again for everyone, George.'

Robin, bland as a snowman and grinning, bought drinks for both men. 'Merry Christmas,' they said warily.

'And jolly holly berries to you.' Robin left them and sat down by Hugh. 'And holly pricks, too,' he muttered, but he had cheered up. 'So what are you doing for the festive season, Hugh—the chairman's wife?'

Hugh attempted to hush him, and his own voice became so quiet that my father only just heard him say, 'I don't think I rate with Lady Lockyer. I don't have the social standing.'

'But something extremely tasty has been seen nipping up the museum steps. More than once.'

'If she's the one I think you mean, she's just a girl doing a bit of research.'

'Randy museum chief's secret love nest,' said Robin.

'Keep your voice down,' said Hugh. 'You don't think I'm going to wreck a budding career for a girl, do you?'

'Stuffed birds not just in glass cases.'

'What do I have to do to shut you up?'

'Try bribery.' Robin had an empty glass, but one of the men at the bar had seen it and it was filled before Hugh got the chance.

'And I'll tell you something else, Robin, before it comes to you by a devious route. I took her to King John's Lakes—and I only did *that* because I had a phone call from Mr Puckeridge.'

'I hope you held your breath, old boy.'

'He was asking me about the Lakes. He wanted a bit of background, some historical stuff, so I went out to take a look. OK?'

'OK by me. The Puke always gets somebody to do the legwork.'

'It seems he's about to run some story about the Lakes. He was quite excited.'

114

'Well, he would be, wouldn't he?'

'And as the young lady in question happens to have an interest in certain aspects of the Lakes I took her along with me. And to damp down those steamy thoughts that afflict you, I'll tell you she's a schoolgirl, so it's all utterly above board.'

'As she's a schoolgirl.'

Hugh sighed. 'Platonic,' he said. 'Utterly. In spite of her looks.'

At the mention of a schoolgirl, my father's ears pricked up. He and my mother later spent hours wondering who it could be, but at the time there was a new twist to what Hugh and Robin were saying, and Hugh was obviously glad to get away from the subject of the girl. He could not understand why the newspaper was so interested in King John's Lakes, and he asked Robin what was behind it.

'Me,' said Robin. 'I'm behind it. It's me who's got the Puke all worked up.'

'Over what exactly?'

'The Lakes are going to be sold. Somebody's after 'em.'

My father rather agreed with Hugh when he said, 'Sold. Is that all?'

'It's got the Puke dribbling all over his desk. He's giving it the works—page one lead, four-column picture, the lot.'

'So somebody's going to buy a bit of wasteland. Why didn't you say? What's so secret?'

'Ah, but Hugh, *who* is going to buy the land? And why? And for what purpose?'

'Should I know? Does it matter?'

'The Puke doesn't know, either. So he's got a mystery on his hands, hasn't he? He's in top gear—investigative journalism at its frightening best. But quite safe, you understand. Mr Puckeridge would not want to upset anybody. We're just printing the rumour.'

'It might upset old Josh Lovegrove.'

'Don't worry about Josh. When I write it up I'm going to give him a "no comment".'

'And you're not even going to see him, am I right?'

'No need, old boy.'

'There is something insufferably complacent about you, my devious Robin. What deep game are you playing?'

'I've given my little Pukey his Christmas lead story all gift-wrapped and sanitized. Nothing unpleasant to alarm him.'

'And handed to him by Robin Redbreast.'

'Very droll, Hugh.'

'So where's the catch?'

'No catch. No catch at all.' Robin drank. 'All I'll admit to, Hugh, is that I'm putting down a little bait to bring the rats out into the open.'

'What rats?'

Robin shrugged, but now it was he who kept his voice low. 'I just think that people ought to know who it is who wants to buy the Lakes,' he said.

'And you know already.'

'Maybe yes, maybe no. But one thing the Puke would never do would be to print the names I've got—so I'm not going to put him in the embarrassing position of having to screw his little brains up to decide.'

'He's your editor. I thought you had to tell him everything.'

'I wouldn't want to spoil his Christmas, would I?'

'So who is it who wants to buy out old Josh Lovegrove? And how do *you* know about it?'

Robin once again raised his voice to call across the room, 'Mum's the word, George.'

The barman regarded him gravely. 'Mum's the word, sir.'

It was exasperating for my father. He didn't know the name of the girl who visited the museum, and he had no

116

idea who was trying to buy the Lakes—even though the two men at the bar were Julian Green and Lacey Lockyer.

21 Suspicion

Virginia gets more satisfaction out of writing than she does from *anything* else. She told me so—or rather, she wrote to me about it. We wrote a great deal once we found out about each other.

It began when I got Harry riled that day in the common room and Charlotte suddenly had the idea that she and Harry could write their own love story. Of course she told Virginia about it, and about the skinny boy who had butted in and seemed to become part of the story. Virginia was on to me like a flash. She recognized another writer.

Virginia writes because she can never keep anything to herself. She says that writing is like talking to someone who is even better than your best friend, because the paper you write on doesn't answer back, or whisper to someone else, or look at you and make you blush after you've confessed even the worst things.

And then you give it to someone to read, I said.

Only the best bits, said Virginia.

Which is how I came to know so much about Charlotte that only a girl would know. She must have concocted some things, but so do I. You can't get at the truth without fiction. Virginia got carried away when Charlotte was in a turmoil over Harry and Hugh Beamish and she hardly knew how to stop writing— and she was enthralled by any hint of mystery, such as the time when Charlotte first suspected that her brother was spying on King John's Lakes.

117

This was the day that Charlotte ran away from the warehouse and found herself having coffee with Hugh Beamish. She was late getting home, and her mother was annoyed and asked her where she'd been.

'Just up town,' said Charlotte.

'Your tea's on the table, what there is. We just about finished.'

Derek was gazing across the table towards the television in the corner, and the room seemed suddenly to crowd in on Charlotte. She said, 'Could we have the telly off, do you think?'

'Why?' said her mother.

'Nobody's really watching. It hurts my eyes.'

'That's a new one—hurts your eyes. And how d'you know nobody's watching, you've only just this minute walked in the door. We been watching something, Derek and me, ain't we, Derek? It don't hurt *our* eyes. It never did harm to anybody's eyes. That's been proved.'

'It doesn't matter.' Charlotte looked down at the plates. Hardly any two were alike. The sliced bread was collapsing in its packet like the pages of an open book, and the lid of the pickle jar lay near the brown smear on Derek's plate.

'Not good enough for you?' Her mother had read her glance, and her small, vindictive face was raised, sniffing for prey. 'First it's telly, now it's the way we eat. I suppose I shouldn't have asked him in, that young feller when he called, but he said he didn't have time. If he'd come through the door he'd a seen the way we live, and then where would you a bin, Lady Muck of Turd Hall?'

'Mother.' Derek, at ease, one elbow on the table, and his chest digesting its first lungful of cigarette, spoke without lifting his gaze from the screen. 'You got to admit your viewing is a bit unselective.'

Silence. Charlotte looked into her lap.

'A bit unselective,' Derek inhaled again, 'like the vast majority of the population. You got to admit it's been proved over and over again by the mass media that when it comes to the on-off switch the viewing public don't know its arse from its elbow.'

It had happened again. Derek's authority, whenever he cared to use it, could pour oil on his mother's temper even though the sharp eyes still sparked in her daughter's direction.

'Well, she's getting above herself. She didn't want that young feller to come around here after her this afternoon, I can see that.'

'Which young feller is that?' Derek turned towards Charlotte.

'I don't know,' she said hastily. He had caught her off guard.

'It was the boy Green,' said her mother. 'I wish I *had* got him in here after all. That would've spoilt your chances, wouldn't it, if he'd seen your mother was watching telly in the middle of the afternoon?'

Derek said, 'Turn it off, Mother, while we're talking.'

She reached out and stabbed at the switch. 'If that's what you want,' she said, 'that's what you got. Now what you got to say?' There was silence. 'See? Bloody marvellous conversation we got now.'

Derek paid her no attention and she got to her feet to begin clearing the table, clashing the plates.

Derek spoke to the air in the middle of the room. 'I've got to ring a business acquaintance tonight.'

'Pity you sold your car,' said his mother. 'You could've gone to see him.'

'The nature of our business is such that it's got to be telephonic communication.' His small eyes, like two black spots on a dice, settled for a second on Charlotte. 'Are you wi' me?'

She did not understand him, so she reached for the teapot before her mother removed it and poured herself a cup. 'It's a pity we're not on the phone,' she said, 'then you wouldn't have to go out in the cold.'

119

'My little sister always was considerate,' he said.

'Excuse me while I'm sick,' said his mother.

Derek tapped ash into his saucer. 'He's a nice young chap is that boy Green. Funny he should've come here this afternoon, because his father moves in the circles I'm connected with, if you follow me.' Again the flick of the eye-dice. 'Which is why I referred to that phone call I got to make.'

Derek was hardly ever as friendly as this and it made her uncomfortable. 'Oh,' she said.

'There's a big land deal going on. Very big—well, to be honest with you, *quite* big for Weldelph, and I got reason to believe that Mr Green Senior, that's his father, is going to be one of the principal executors.'

'Executors?' said Mrs Bush. 'Is somebody dead, then?'

'Mother, why don't you get into the scullery with them dishes?'

'Executors is when somebody's dead. I had that with your father when he passed on. Executors is when there's a will.'

'Ma, executor was a partial mistake. A slip of the tongue. What I was thinking of was collaborationist. Mr Green is a business collaborationist.'

'Probate,' she said. 'That's wills as well. But you should know all about that because that's what they gave you that first time you got into trouble—probate.'

'I was on *probation*, Ma! Them buggers put me on probation.' He was sweating as he looked at his sister. 'For something I never done, Char, but I was only young at the time.'

'You was generous in them days, Derek. You always gave us something from whatever it was you got. And you kept yourself in shirts ever since you was quite small. I never see so many white shirts as you had that first time they come with a warrant.'

'Yes, Ma.'

'I know they wasn't all yours, that was what the trouble was all about.'

'Ma, I was just looking after them for someone. Remember? It all came out later.'

'Probate, that's what they done to you that time.'

'Switch the telly on. I know there's one of your programmes.' He looked at the ceiling. 'There bleedin' well better be.'

'I got to clear the table for her ladyship.'

'No.' Charlotte got to her feet. 'I'll do it. I want to do it.'

'Sit down.' Derek reached for her with one hand while he lowered his forehead into the palm of the hand that held the cigarette. 'Sit down. Sit down.' He shook his head and ash fell on the plumply padded rolls of his pullover. 'My life ain't never followed a primrose path, Charlotte. Misunderstandings have frogmarched my heeltaps all the way.'

A burst of bright chatter came from the television and he raised his head. 'Even that is music to my ears, Charlotte,' he said, 'after the places I've been.'

Sympathy for him flooded her and she said, 'I know, Derek. Things haven't always gone right for you.'

He detected the change in her and became confident. 'There's nothing crooked about this deal, Charlotte. Nothing questionable at all. Well there wouldn't be; I'm only on the fringes, as it were, in a sort of advisory capacity. And I got reason to suspect,' he lowered his voice below the level of the telly sound, 'that it's to do with King John's Lakes, are you wi' me?'

'No,' she said quickly, 'I'm not.'

'Well, you know the Lakes, girl, and you know old Josh Lovegrove. You must have been there.'

'No,' she lied. 'I know where they are, but I've never been there.'

The little eyes flicked up and remained steady. 'That ain't what I heard.'

121

'Well, I suppose I have. But not for a long time. Not recently.' It was easy enough to lie to him. It was what he expected.

'I'll be honest wi' you, Charlotte. My associates in this deal have got funny little minds and I don't like being mixed up with anything that ain't fair and square and above board, you know that.'

'I know that, Derek.'

'I'm your brother when all's said and done. And I always looked after you ever since you was knee-high to a grasshopper, ain't I?' His eyes were on her and held steady. 'Well, knee-high to a pretty big grasshopper, I admit.'

He laughed, but his eyes probed into hers, seeking to know something. She was puzzled. 'You always gave me things when I was a kid,' she said. He occasionally had given her a present.

'I'm glad you can acknowledge that, Charlotte. And I ain't seeking for you to pay off a debt or anything, but you might be in a position to give your brother a bit of help. Right?' He had spent a lot of time working up to it, and now he spoke quickly. 'What I want to know— well, what my *associates* want to know, is whether that old bugger Josh ...' He broke off and drew deeply on his cigarette. 'Is whether Mr Lovegrove is only selling his land, or if there's something else.'

'Selling?' Charlotte's surprise betrayed her. She felt herself redden as she shrugged, pretending to be indifferent. 'Selling, is he?'

'You know something about it?'

She shook her head.

'I thought maybe young Green let something slip,' he said.

'I don't know him that well, now do I, Derek?'

'I don't know how well you know anybody, Charlotte.' He seemed pained, as though she had kept

122

something from him. 'But you ain't a bad-looking girl. I've heard people say you was pretty. There's at least one gentleman in this town who thinks you're *beautiful*, and if a beautiful girl don't get to know things, then she's got to be beautiful *and* stupid. Which you ain't. Are you wi' me?'

She sat silent. They did not look at each other.

'Your brother needs all the help he can get,' Derek said. 'And if a beautiful girl can't give him a bit of information then she ain't got a heart.'

'She ain't.' Her mother spoke over Charlotte's shoulder. 'She ain't got a heart for you, Derek, you can bank on that, because she ain't got a heart for her own mother.'

'All I want to know,' he said, 'is who's kidding who. Them Lakes, for instance, they're only a bit of swampy old rubbish, ain't they?'

'How would I know?' said Charlotte.

'You might. But never mind that. What if there was something else?'

'What do you mean something else?'

'I mean some secret invention. Some machinery that old Josh Lovegrove has got so he don't have to bother about making a livelihood if anybody should take the Lakes off of him. Are you wi' me now?' She shook her head, and he leant across the table. 'Because I been led to believe there is something strange going on. I been led to believe there's a bit of delicate machinery that moves by itself. And I believe there's money in that for whoever gets in first.'

She knew she had gone pale. She pushed her chair back so quickly she shook the table.

'Look what you done,' said her mother. 'You slopped your tea.'

Charlotte was on her feet. 'I don't know what you're getting at, Derek,' she said, 'but I've only once been to the Lakes and then I was with someone else, and old Mr

123

Lovegrove wasn't at home so we came away. We didn't see anything at all, nothing unusual.'

He could see that she was being honest, and now it was he who was puzzled. He spoke more to himself than to her. 'Maybe I'm the only one who knows,' he said. He looked up. 'Sorry I spoke, Charlie girl. I must've made a mistake.'

'Never mind.' She backed out of the room. 'I'm going out tonight. I've got to get ready.'

'Where are you going?' Her mother rarely wanted to know.

'There's a disco.' It was the end-of-term thing. She had not been keen, but now it would be a refuge.

Her mother was sour. 'I expect he'll be there, that young feller you don't want here.'

'He might be.' Charlotte made her escape but, before the door closed, her mother was speaking to Derek.

'Toffee-nosed little bitch,' she said, 'she'll get what's coming to her one o' these days.'

22 The Disco

If Virginia can put me in one of her stories—which she has—it may seem strange that we have never touched each other. With us, it was words, even at the disco. We had taken time out and were standing in the corridor with Trigger when he said, 'All those bodies—seething with streptococci.'

'And worse,' she said. 'People are falling in love.'

'I thought you liked love stories, Virginia,' I said, but she rounded on me.

'Don't be stupid, Williams. There's no such thing as love in my stories. I won't allow it.'

124

It was one of her tricks to take people by surprise. I had played along with the idea that the people in her stories must have been in love to do what they did. There was every contortion of pleasure you could think of, but she'd suddenly made me realize there was one thing that never happened. In her stories people never surrendered. Even though they gave in over and over again and did what people wanted them to do, none of them ever surrendered in the way that Charlotte had wanted to surrender and be in Harry's story. But that was love.

'You're right,' I said. 'Love is too difficult to write about.'

I knew that sort of comment would appeal to Trigger, which was why I'd said it; partly. We were in the corridor outside the common room but there was a window through which we could see the coloured lights raking the dancers and flickering in the fug of the music.

'It's Christmas,' said Trigger, 'the traditional time for diseases, suicide and beheadings.'

'Tiny Tim,' said Virginia.

'Sir Gawain and the Green Knight.'

'Robins with bloody breasts.'

'And Scrooge,' I said.

'That lovely man,' said Virginia and held out a plastic cup into which Trigger poured her a drink from a flat bottle. 'Here's to hollow rooms and the rattle of chains on bare floorboards, the true spirit of Christmas. He made one mistake, you know.'

'Who did?' he asked. 'Are you drunk, Virginia?'

'You hope I am, you in your allegedly sexy black shirt and your tinkly-winkly gold chain. It matches the rim of your glasses, you cunning beast, and makes you almost irresistible. What was the question?'

'You were going to tell me who made a mistake.'

'Scrooge did, you loon. One single, solitary error

125

ruined his entire life, and I can't believe that you, Trigger darling, don't know what that is. And it wasn't because he was stingy, although you know plenty about that as well.' She held out her cup again, but he shook his head, grinning. 'What big teeth you've got,' she said.

'That's because I'm a wolf in wolf's clothing.'

'How strange, then, that I feel my virginity is not at risk in your company.'

'Nor is mine,' he said, 'in yours,' and his laughter came snuffling through his grin.

By this time I was out of it, a mere spectator. Virginia was watching Trigger over the rim of her cup.

'And what big eyes *you*'ve got,' he said.

'All the better to suss you out.' She wore a white shirt in contrast to his black, and tight trousers of dazzling pink. She stood nursing her cup in front of her stomach, stockily, like a soldier, her feet slightly apart. 'The mistake that Scrooge made,' she said, 'was that he fell in love, and he should never have done that. Money was much more important to him than girls. He got all slushy at the end and betrayed himself. Please don't make the same mistake, Trigger my sweet.'

'I shall stick to money. It is easier to understand.'

'Don't go in for girls whatever you do.'

'I won't.'

'I know you won't. I wish I could say the same.' She held out her cup and he took the bottle from inside his shirt and poured. She turned to look through the window into the dim turmoil of the disco. 'Do you ever have the feeling that you know too much, Trigger?'

'I know I know too much.'

'I mean without being clever. Everybody knows too much—we're all going to die, and that's far too much, but it doesn't *hurt*. Not like . . .' She put both elbows on the ledge of the corridor window and, with her face against the glass, gazed at the movement inside. 'Not like being fond of someone—*fond*, know what I mean?

head-over-heels fond—and knowing all the time that they're not matching you, fond for fond.'

'The veil in the eyes,' said Trigger. 'The veil that stays down.'

She was silent for a moment. 'I wish I'd said that,' she said. 'It would have eased the pain. Oh, Trigger, just look at her!'

An amber beam skimmed the dancers and their hair flared like sunset clouds. Charlotte was in white, a loose blouson to the waist and then close-fitting white trousers. She was moving so slightly that at first she seemed to be standing still, but then I saw that she was breasting the beat of the music like a sea swimmer, not yet out of her depth but playing to the swell, letting it lift her so that her feet stroked the sand with no weight. And then she stood firm, resisting the suck of the sound until she allowed the next wave to sway her. She had surrendered to it only in order to ride it.

'In pure white,' Virginia sighed. 'The snow maiden.'

'Her bottom's too big,' he said.

'She's not one of your boys, darling, with bums all muscle and hollows, and equipment bunched up at the front.'

'It's a question of taste.'

'O Lord, Trigger, I know!' She swung away from the window, her eyes wide. 'And who can blame other people for wanting her? But she's a kind of dream. You've only got to try to touch her and she goes away from you, she's not there.'

Trigger put a finger on the bridge of his glasses, pushed them higher on his nose and gazed beyond her into the room. 'I wonder,' he said, 'if everybody comes away from her empty-handed. That one, for instance.'

'Oh, that one.' She had followed his gaze. 'Harry Green is just another dream-chaser. He's way out of his depth, did he but know it.'

'Surely,' said Trigger, 'he's one of your hollow-but-

127

tocked good-lookers. Blondish sort of hair and a face that some might like to look upon, a bit heavy maybe, but not dull, not bourgeois.'

'Harry Green *not* bourgeois? My mother knows his mother, my absent father used to know his father, and Harry isn't only bourgeois, he's *Weldelph*. Poor Harry, apart from a quite pretty mouth in that slab of a face he hasn't got much going for him, not from her point of view.'

'Money?'

'It embarrasses her. She's shy because she hasn't got any, and she blushes when she thinks about his daddy's big warehouse. It frightens her. So does Daddy.'

'He frightens most people around here. He'll scare her off if he wants to.'

'And don't you wish he would, Trigger my pet?'

'Don't you?'

She held his eyes for a long moment before she turned away and suddenly recollected that I was alongside them. She grinned at me. 'We know his father's got nothing to worry about, don't we, John Williams? Charlotte is not going to steal his little boy away. He's far too young.' She leant forward and lowered her voice as if she didn't want Trigger to overhear. 'Poor old Trigger. He doesn't know about the older man in her life; handsome Hugh, the molester of schoolgirls.'

She did not allow Trigger to question her but turned back to the window. 'What are they saying to each other, those two?' she asked.

'Even if you don't know now,' I said, 'you'll find out later.'

'As if it mattered.' Trigger gave one of his superior, snickering laughs. 'Anyone can see that poor old Charlotte is quite bereft of brains.'

Her gaze was vacant because she was dancing with Harry but thinking of Hugh. She told Virginia she couldn't prevent the man's face in the after-shave ad on telly coming into her mind, and it reminded her of Hugh. She let her eyelids droop and concentrated on the music, but the beat made a silver shiver of lights in her head, like the man's brown face and shoulders splashed with glittering droplets. She opened her eyes and saw Harry. His face was pale.

'Charlie,' he said.

'Don't call me that.' It was easy, wrapped around by music, to say whatever she liked.

'Sorry,' he said.

She tilted her head and her hair surged on her shoulder. She posed like an ad girl. He tried to stop her. Hold her still.

'I want to tell you something, Charlotte.'

'Tell me, then.'

'Not here.'

She saw him frown, moving against the beat like a bad swimmer defying the ocean. 'You've got a young kid's face, Harry. You're like a really young kid.'

He reached and grabbed her hand.

'Let me go!'

'You've got to come with me. I want to tell you something.'

Her hair spread as Harry lurched, tugging her after him, and her neck arched and her lips parted. Girl in an ad. Girl on a beach. Girl on white sand. She heard her heels clatter, out of time with the music, cheap.

Out in the corridor, 'Please,' he said.

She eased her fingers from his grip. School smell. And after-shave. Trigger was wearing it. 'Well, hullo there,' said Trigger, and his teeth grew large, but Harry walked past him into the dimness of the corridor and waited for Charlotte. Trigger bowed towards her as she went by.

'My father.' Harry's voice echoed ahead of them into the blackness of the school shut down for Christmas. 'He was terrible with you when we were in his office.'

'Doesn't matter.'

'I've had a big row with him. I don't think the same as he does, not about anything.'

'It doesn't matter, Harry. Damn these heels!' She kicked off her shoes and stooped to pick them up. 'I can't stand the clatter.'

'Charlotte, I shouldn't have let you run away. I didn't know why you did it. I didn't realize till afterwards. I hate him for that.'

'It wasn't your father. It was the other one. He's a lot worse.'

Now they were walking silently in the stone corridor.

'Charlotte.'

'Yes.'

'I called round to see you this afternoon.'

'I know.'

'But you were down at the Lakes,' he said. 'You were with that museum guy. In his car.'

'I knew there was another car there, but I didn't see you.' She panicked. It was as though Harry had been reading her thoughts.

'You didn't see anybody. You kept combing your hair.'

She laughed, and immediately became cunning. 'It's that stupid grasshopper thing,' she said. 'He wanted Mr Lovegrove to show him the poster you told him about.' She shrugged, confident of herself now. 'But we were wasting our time because old Josh wasn't there anyway.'

They had turned a corner. Pale squares of windows lined one wall of the corridor and made it into a mysterious colonnade where, not long ago, he would have reached for her and they would have kissed. Now he made no movement towards her, and it was she who leant forward until their lips touched. 'Don't be angry, Harry.'

'I'm not.'

'Well, you should be.' Suddenly it was she who was angry with him for not flying into a rage. He had seen

130

her with another man, why wasn't he white-hot with anger? Why didn't he hate her? She deserved to be hated. She yearned for it.

She pushed herself away from him and stooped to put on her shoes.

'Charlotte?' he said.

'What?'

'I called to see you this afternoon because I wanted to ask you something.'

He spoke timidly, and this increased her anger. She waited.

'Tomorrow,' he said. 'Can I see you tomorrow?'

'Why?'

'I'm going to see Josh Lovegrove.'

'Big deal.'

'I was wondering if you'd come with me.'

'Why should I?'

'Because I want to find out why he needs that stuff my father gave him.'

'Stuff?'

'That American Gut.'

Her laughter burst out. 'American Gut!' she cried. 'That's the nicest thing you've said to me all evening!'

'I'm sorry.' He hung his head.

'Damn you, Harry Green,' she said. 'Damn you, damn you,' but she held his hand and led him back to the disco.

23 The Barn

A robin placed his dot of orange among the humps of frosted snow in the brambles, and Charlotte knew she was caught in the picture on a Christmas card. The foreground was the gate in the ragged hedge and beyond

131

it was the broken ground of the middle distance, simplified by snow, and then the grey stretches of frozen ponds and lakes. Beyond, stretching far away but never climbing more than a third of the way up the picture, lay the flat horizon tinged with the pink and yellow of a winter sunset. A glint of a star high in the sky perfected it.

They stood, straddling their cycles, as Harry leant over to lift the frozen latch.

'Dark soon,' she said. There was a paper stillness in the air and her words hardly carried. 'I hope he's here.'

'He will be.' Snow sifted from the bars as Harry pushed the gate open. 'He said any time today.'

She rode past him. 'I can't stay long, don't forget.'

'Why is that?' he asked.

She did not answer. She cycled ahead of him, deeper into the Christmas card. Her tyres crackled in the icy ruts as though she was creasing a page of stiff paper, and the bushes, weighted white for winter, folded around her.

'It took me long enough to find you today,' he called.

'I was out.'

He knew that well enough. 'Where were you?'

'Round and about.' Once more she shut him out.

She watched the spray of snow from her wheels. If I stop, she thought, I shall be fixed here. I'll be a girl painted into the scene. The cold will never end and I shall never cease cycling, and though I am moving I shall never move, and no one who looks at the picture will know who I am because my face is turned away and all they can see is my back.

'I'm not dressed for this,' she said. It was stupid not to have changed after going out to lunch with Hugh Beamish, but Harry had found her at home before she'd had the chance. She bit her lips to remove what was left of her lipstick. Not that it mattered; nothing mattered—not Hugh Beamish acting big in the restaurant in Lynn,

132

nor red-nose Harry trailing behind like a kid. 'I wish you hadn't brought me here,' she said. 'It's stupid.'

'Sorry,' he said. 'I thought you wanted to see if anything's happening.'

'Well, I don't.' Not with him. Not with anybody. Why couldn't they leave her alone?

She almost fell off as she rounded a bend in the bushes. And Joshua Lovegrove was more stupid than anybody. He was mad. His ridiculous home faced her now. A veranda and a narrow strip of garden ran alongside the railway carriage. Some of the blinds were down, but through other windows she could see the corridor and the brass rail that protected the glass, and at one end a little chimney threw out a plume of white smoke which drifted along the length of the roof so that, for a moment, it seemed that the old carriage was on its tracks and moving again. But it had no wheels. Nothing moved without wheels.

'Well,' she said, 'where is he?'

Harry rested his bike against the carriage and walked along the veranda knocking on doors and looking through windows without response. 'He's here all right,' he said.

'How do you know?'

'Because of that.' He pointed to where old Josh's thin cane hung from a handgrip near one of the doors and he laughed. 'He never goes far without it.'

'What's funny?'

'I thought you knew.'

'Well, I don't,' and she glanced away, not wanting him to say anything. 'You'd better go and take a look over there.'

The barn stood well back among the white bushes, as big and black as a railway shed. He saw footprints leading to it through the snow and knew that the old man must be there but he trudged towards it without trying

133

to tell her. He had never seen her like this; so angry with everything. Her face was enamel, smooth and hard.

The planks of the barn overlapped like the sides of a boat and were thickly tarred. The footprints curved away towards the door, but a window was closer and he made for it. She saw him stoop to the glass and shield his eyes against the reflection. Then he was still.

'Hurry up,' she muttered. 'I'm freezing.'

She watched him straighten, turn and beckon to her. She sighed, let her bike fall sideways into the snow, and went over to him. This was utterly childish.

'I can't make it out,' he said, 'but there's something there.'

It was dark within the barn but Charlotte, peering through the cave made by her hands, could see a structure in the centre of the floor. She sighed again. 'It looks like a model ship to me,' she said. Within the cradle of struts there was a boat shape. 'I suppose that's what he wants the gut for, the rigging or something.'

Harry looked again. 'Maybe,' he said. But the boat shape could be something else; the fuselage of an aeroplane. He strained his eyes. It was very small for an aircraft, not even big enough for a microlite. His mind, for some reason, went no further than aeroplanes or boats.

'If that's all there is to see,' she said, 'I'm going.' She saw he was disappointed, but it was easy to be cruel to him. And there was pleasure in it. 'I haven't got much time, anyway.'

'I'd still like to see what it is,' he said.

He was like a kid getting excited over a toy. She turned away.

'Aren't you going to wait?'

'No.'

The cold pricked her eyes and she did not at first see that the door of the barn had opened. Under the bobble hat Josh Lovegrove was smiling and speaking to her.

'An interesting device, don't you think, young lady?'

'Fascinating,' she said briefly and hunched her shoulders and stamped her feet to demonstrate how cold she was. Old Josh instantly tugged off his cap and bowed her inside. 'You too, young felluar; there's no shortage of space.'

Harry, waiting for Charlotte to kick the snow from her shoes, was impatient. 'Is the American Gut the sort you want?' he asked. 'Does it work?'

But Josh was watching Charlotte as she entered the barn. 'Oh,' she cried, 'a stove!'

It stood on its stone pedestal and was so hot that its fat body glowed a dull red in the dimness of the barn. She made straight for it and stood beside it, warming herself and ignoring the structure in the centre of the floor. The door shut. Harry smelt the hot iron but glanced only briefly at the stove. He could see now what was kept in the barn. It was a canoe, and not very big. The cradle that held it seemed too elaborate. 'Much more to do?' he asked Josh.

'The stringing is well-nigh completed.'

'Oh, the stringing.' But Harry was puzzled. 'Stringing?' he said.

'My Uncle Cox left clear instructions.' Josh had unhooked an oil lamp from the wall and was lighting it.

Charlotte heard their voices behind her but was too busy absorbing the warmth of the stove to pay them much heed. It was not until she heard Josh strike the match that she turned her head. What she saw made her cry out.

'Harry!'

He twisted towards her.

'Look out!'

She took a pace forward, pointing at something behind him, and he twisted again to look back.

It seemed to be a horse with huge eyes and a ragged mouth. Harry stepped back. Its head nodded in the

135

flicker of the lamplight, and he took another step backwards, stumbled and fell. It was then he saw that the horse was a gigantic grasshopper. He could see its underparts, its plated keel, and its bolt-cutter mouth as it appeared to stride towards him on thin legs. He rolled away and a rope coil on the floor caught at his foot. He dragged himself backwards but a nightmare, something that belonged to sleep, followed him in daylight. His foot was gripped and moved with a slowness no effort could quicken.

He stretched back, reaching for Charlotte's hand to haul himself clear, but at that moment the lantern illuminated Josh's face. The little man grinned in the gleam of his stubble.

'Get up, Harry.' It was Charlotte who recovered first. 'It's not real.' She looked uncertainly towards the old man. 'It isn't real, is it, Mr Lovegrove?'

'On the contrary,' he said. 'It is genuine.'

'You know what I mean.' Fright had made her sharp. 'It's not a real grasshopper. It can't be.'

Harry, freeing himself from the soft rope around his ankle, gazed at the creature. 'Cox's Animals!' he said suddenly. 'I knew it! They *do* exist!'

'I must disappoint you there.' Josh swung his lantern towards it. 'Only one exists. There was never another.'

Harry stood up. 'So it has to be the one in the photograph.' He took a step nearer, and saw the faint light of the windows reflected in the sheen of its green plates. 'But it's beautiful, Josh! It's perfect!'

Charlotte watched him walk closer before she followed. Just behind its head there was a saddle of dark green velvet and she was afraid he would attempt to climb on its back, but he did no more than stroke it, admiring it. Its limbs seemed too slender to support more than its own weight. The front legs were angled forward, and their complicated claws touched the floorboards with a delicacy that made her shudder. 'It won't

136

attack me, will it?' She looked back, smiling at old Josh, wanting him to reassure her. 'It won't eat me?'

'It has an appetite for this alone.' He stooped and picked up a strand of the rope that had tripped Harry. 'American Gut,' he said.

It was whitish and of an uneven thickness. 'I don't like the look of that,' she said.

'I have been warming it into suppleness,' said Josh.

Harry stepped between the legs to the creature's side. Its back was level with his shoulders, and its great back legs made pointed arches above his head too high for him to reach. It was machinery. One of its hinged plates was raised and he could see the complexities of its interior. This had never been an animal on a roundabout; it was much more than that. But what did it do?

'My Uncle Cox despised the wheel.' Josh had come up behind him. 'If God had intended us to run about on wheels, he used to say, he'd have given us smooth highways.' He held up his lantern and swung it. 'But God loved the pendulum and he hung them everywhere. The pendulum wags the world. Hence this great green grasshopper with a pendulum in its belly.'

'To make it jump?' said Harry.

'That was my uncle's theory—when the parts were connected correctly with this.' He prodded at the coils on the floor. 'A natural substance to convert the natural sway of its rider into a leap that would astonish the world.'

'Did it work?'

'My uncle,' said Josh, 'offered a reward for anyone who could ride it.'

Harry, remembering the poster, nodded.

'It was never claimed,' said Josh.

137

24 The Cup Shatters

My mother is just as ridiculous about money as my father. I have to admit that, compared to them, I'm a hoarder—somebody has to be, and I think they're going to be glad to have me around in their old age. I can see them when they're eighty coming to me to borrow the odd fiver like a pair of teenagers. I know they will. Of course, it's working the other way at the moment, and not only with money. I borrow other things from them; mainly people.

There's the Hugh Beamish connection, for instance. They got to know him because of me and the museum, but I was soon on the sidelines. My mother is mixed up in so many projects that Hugh Beamish could hardly escape her, anyway—not that he wanted to. My mother is like me, she's a listener, and people pour out their problems to her—especially the clever ones like Hugh Beamish who you'd expect to look after their own affairs a bit better. He even wrote to her after his disgrace so she wouldn't think so badly of him. I've seen the letter. He tries to make out he had no choice in what he did, and he says a lot about Charlotte, but not much about that particular day when they were alone in the museum together. It was Charlotte who told Virginia all about that, which is how I got to know what happened. I take after my mother in another way; I'm inquisitive, and I didn't let up until Virginia had told me every detail.

It was just after Charlotte and Harry had first seen the grasshopper. She had gone straight from King John's Lakes to see Hugh Beamish at the museum. 'When they started messing about with that horrible gut,' she told him, 'I left.'

He leant against the desk and looked down at her as she crouched close to the gas fire. He thought even her grimace was attractive. 'Extraordinary,' he said.

She looked up and agreed. 'Isn't it.'

She thought he was talking about the grasshopper, and he corrected her. 'It's you, I mean,' he said. 'You are extraordinary, not that big tin toy.'

'But you weren't there, Hugh. You didn't see it.' She turned to face the fire again, knowing that its glow would hide her own redness. 'I thought you'd be interested to hear about it, that's all.'

'I'll go there tomorrow, Charlotte. I'll make him an offer.'

'So that the museum can have it?'

'More for my own benefit. I want to gloat over it.'

'Anyone would think this was your private collection.'

'When that front door closes, Charlotte, it is. It's all mine. I come down and look at it in the night.'

'I don't know how you could.' She thought of his flat upstairs, and the huge darkness of the museum galleries beneath it at night. 'I couldn't wander about among all those stuffed birds.' The birds were not what frightened her most. She was thinking more of the stone coffin that lay open in one dim corner, but it was less shaming to admit being afraid of something not so obvious. 'What if they should start fluttering inside their glass cases?' She shuddered, hearing stiff feathers scrape against glass, and Hugh laughed at her.

'I came down and wandered about in the dark last night, Charlotte. Do you want to know why?'

'No,' she said. 'I don't.'

'Because I was thinking of you.'

She remained silent, listening to the fire whinny in its red pipes.

139

'Charlotte.' She heard him move away from the desk, and she stood up. 'I believe I love you, Charlotte.'

She laughed at that because she always did. It was a game they had begun to play.

'I would love you, Charlotte, if you'd allow me.'

'You'd love that big green grasshopper more if you saw it,' she said. 'I'll take you to the Lakes, even though old Josh Lovegrove probably doesn't like me any more.'

'How do you know?' Hugh had come closer.

'Well, he can't like me. I didn't want to go to see him at his stupid old Lakes, and I let it show.' She stepped back but he was close enough to reach her hand and hold it. She made no effort to get free. It was part of the game. 'You wouldn't have liked me either. I was bitchy.'

'I got out of bed and walked through the galleries.'

'Where are you going to put the grasshopper? It doesn't work, you know. He said so.'

'Even the mummy's hand,' he said. It was from a dead girl, as brown as dry twigs in its glass case. 'I looked at that.'

'The grasshopper,' she said, 'nobody ever managed to ride it.'

'Her fingernails are still painted. I think she must have been beautiful.' Hugh stood in front of her. 'But that was in Egypt. And a long time ago.'

The only lamp in the room was on the desk. It shed a deceitful light from under its shade and, as Hugh came closer, she almost let their lips touch.

'What if somebody should come in?' she said.

'It's Mrs Frost's day off, and anyway she's Christmas shopping, and anyway it's nearly closing time so who the hell is going to climb the steps of Weldelph Museum?'

'Only me.'

'Then take your coat off.' He helped her. 'And kiss me.'

She glanced towards the tall windows and the square

beyond where every horizontal surface was eider-downed in white, and she allowed herself to be drawn towards the bookcases in the corner. He was very tall and she had to tilt her face up. 'I'll pull you down to my level,' she said, and reached up to put her hands each side of his head and bring his face closer. She parted her lips for him.

'Would you like me to give you this museum?' he said, close to her ear. 'It's all yours.' He kissed her again.

'You promised me Napoleon,' she said. 'That's what I came for.'

'Napoleon?'

'I'd still be down at the Lakes if you hadn't told me about Napoleon.'

'Oh, Napoleon!' Suddenly he remembered. 'Just let me lock up.'

He fetched the keys from his desk drawer and she followed him into the foyer where he closed the shutters over the windows and locked the front doors. They went together through the open arch and walked through the galleries to the rear of the museum calling out 'Closing time!' and switching off lights. Their voices echoed in the empty halls. 'There's not even an Egyptian girl lingering here,' he said.

'Don't say things like that.' She shuddered and, just as he was about to put his arms around her, she again reminded him. 'Napoleon.'

He bowed. 'I am yours to command, Empress Josephine.'

'That's cheap,' she said. 'Josephine was cheap.' He sounded like somebody on the telly trying to be funny.

He straightened, and she saw that she had hurt him. Perhaps it was just as well. She felt safer.

He had a smaller bunch of keys in his pocket and he selected one and went to a tall exhibition case in the centre of the main gallery. There were many things arranged in tiers behind the glass, a chess set in which

141

the knights were miniature men prancing on horses, nautilus shells set in silver and wantonly displaying their lips of mother of pearl, some huge seals bearing kings' heads, and a tea service of delicate green and white. He unlocked the glass front and swung it open.

'Sèvres china,' he said. 'Captured at Waterloo. That's the very teapot that Boney used.' He lifted it out. 'And we are going to be the first people to drink from it in over a century—and damn Josephine.' He looked up, but she was no longer at his side. 'Charlotte?'

She was at the foot of a short flight of stairs that led to a low landing where the staircase divided to climb to both ends of the open gallery above. 'This would be a good place for the grasshopper,' she said.

'You've got that insect on the brain. Don't you want a cup of Napoleon tea?'

She stood on the platform of the landing where an alabaster Buddha squatted and smiled. 'Old Josh really thinks someone will be able to ride it. Leaping over houses.'

'In that case,' he said, 'it's far better that it should be in here where it won't break anyone's neck. It's an absurd thing for anyone to construct anyway. Why a grasshopper?'

'I've told you. Pendulums. Old Uncle Cox was sure that anybody who was really in harmony with everything and could forget about himself could do it.'

'Like the Buddha beside you.'

She looked down at it. It was far too obvious. 'More like riding a bike,' she said. 'You just don't have to think about it.'

Hugh was silent for a moment. 'But Charlotte,' he said, still thoughtful, 'the idea might have lots of possibilities. Commercial ones, I mean. Just suppose you could harness your own energy so you could vault over a house—there's no telling what you might do.'

'There's only one thing wrong.' She came down the

142

steps. 'Nobody's ever managed to do it. There's no magic left in the world, I suppose you know that, Hugh.'

'I take leave to doubt it, Charlotte. There's magic where you are.'

He made as if to come towards her, but she held up her hand and said, 'Napoleon tea. You promised.'

He looked down at the teapot he was holding and laughed. 'What would Lady Lockyer say if she could see us now? This is a precious exhibit, Charlotte.'

'I don't care. I wish *he* could see it—her horrible husband. I should like him to know just what I am doing at this moment.' She had come forward and picked up a cup. 'I'll smash it.'

'Smash it, then,' he said.

She looked up at him. His black hair had come forward to hang in two points, one touching either cheekbone. It emphasized the intensity of his eyes.

'Shall I?' she asked.

He nodded, and she opened her hand and let the cup fall.

At that moment Harry pushed his bike into the hedge by the Lakes and left it. He needed time to think. Nothing had gone right. It had begun to snow, and words shifted in his mind like falling snowflakes. He watched a single flake descending, appearing first as a dark speck against the fading whiteness of the sky, jostling among other dark fragments and, for a while, not snow at all. Not snow until it was white, and then becoming feathery but in the shapeless shape of a tumbling white rock even though it floated like a feather, a tiny ship of the air, soundless, a sailing island with galleries of crystal, unseen but detectable, fragile as froth, hard as ice, falling to add itself by chance to a bush. And the bush remained a bush but was unseen, shaped by snowflakes.

He stooped to examine it but could not detect his flake among the others. The infinitesimal shock of its landing had been sufficient to fuse its crystals to the crystals beneath and the crystals on every side, and it was now no longer a flake but had sacrificed itself to become part of the landscape of the humped and hidden bush.

'It's gone but not gone,' he said aloud. 'There ought to be a word for not gone. Notgone. Like Charlotte. Charlotte's notgone.'

New snowflakes drifted down without ceasing and, as he walked, he opened his mouth until one arrived on his tongue. 'Charlotte,' he said.

She crouched over the shattered cup and allowed herself to be kissed.

PART FIVE

25 Into the Open

The day the story broke in the *Messenger* my father was in town buying a Christmas present for Mum, which is why he was in the Horse and Groom quite early. He hadn't yet had a chance to read Robin Horn's rumour that King John's Lakes were to be sold to a couple of unnamed business men, which is why he didn't join in when he heard Robin say to the barman, 'The Christmas bells have started to ring, George. They've been tinkling on the Puke's desk all morning.'

'Good tidings, I trust, Mr Horn.'

'He's locked in the bog, George. No more phone calls.'

George smoothed the *Messenger* on the bar and indicated the story on the front page, tapping it with a rubbery fingertip. 'Very nicely put, Mr Horn. My sentiments exactly.' But his wink made Robin shudder.

'Don't do that, George. You look like Rikki-Tikki-Tavi eyeing up a snake.'

'But we've flushed 'em out, Mr Horn. They won't find it so easy now to take advantage of my old mate Josh. He's far too trusting. He needs protecting from himself.' It was a longer speech than George usually indulged in, and he emphasized it with stabs of his finger on the bar. 'You might have saved a decent old chap from being swindled by a couple of sharks, Mr Horn. That sort daren't act out in the open.'

Robin raised his glass and spoke across it. 'You don't like 'em, George. That right?'

'Especially the smooth one, Mr Horn. Especially the consultant. He's the one that needs a nip.'

'And he's the one deepest in the woodwork.' Robin winked at my father, who by this time knew well enough not to ask questions. All he had to do was wait. Robin never played anything very close to his chest for long. Now he said, 'Friend Julian has exposed himself already this morning, George.'

'Not a pretty sight, Mr Horn.'

'Gave the Puke an earful first thing. Filthy rumours, he said. Untrue. Where did the story come from? Poor Pukey shrank and shrank until he was just a little squeak.'

Without being asked to do so, George refilled Robin's glass, and my father's. 'And you observed all this, did you, Mr Horn?'

'Nudge, nudge, George. Alice on the switchboard plugged me in.'

'You have friends in important places, sir.'

'I've protected my rear ever since I was a choirboy, George. But the Puke sold me down the river all the same.'

'How can that be? You told him no names.' He frowned at the *Messenger*. 'And no names are mentioned here.'

'Rest easy, George. He knows nothing about my sources. And never will.'

'No need for you to mention it, Mr Horn. I knew I could rely on you.'

'But the Puke is not the same as other men. When Julian put the pressure on, the Puke told him all he knew.'

'Which wasn't very much, as I understand it.'

'You understand right, George. But the Puke squealed and said it was all his reporter's fault. And he gave away who that reporter was.'

'Not very commendable.' George shook his head.

146

'I pulled the plug on him and walked out. Have a lubricant, George.'

My father, who had turned the paper around on the bar, had got the gist of the *Messenger*'s front page story and guessed that Robin was tangling with some of Weldelph's big boys. 'You're going to need friends, Robin,' he said.

George chipped in. 'Where is the museum gentleman today?' he asked.

'A prior engagement,' said Robin, who seemed glad to get away from the sale of King John's Lakes. 'He warned me he would be busy elsewhere.'

'A certain young lady?' said my father, angling for information about the mysterious schoolgirl who had been seen with Hugh Beamish.

'You could be right,' said Robin, giving nothing away.

My father had not given up. 'He must be very keen on her,' he said.

'Besotted,' said Robin. 'He'd lay down his life for that one.' But then Mr Puckeridge sidled into the bar, his little eyebrows twitching nervously over his glasses, and Robin had other things to think of.

26 A Christmas Drink with the Lockyers

Only a man with a very bad conscience would confess the sort of things that Hugh Beamish wrote to my mother. When she read his letter she was in tears, more for him, I think, than anyone else, even though he made other people suffer. Maybe she's right. He must have seen himself as he really was, and it hurt. Very badly.

What made it even worse for him was that it all began so well, which is what really made Mum cry. He said that as he climbed the steps alongside the bow window

147

of the Lockyers' house and reached to the brass door knocker in the centre of the holly wreath he realized quite suddenly that he was about to enjoy a perfect Christmas. It was true that the summons to the house on The Sweep had arrived late, but there was no denying the friendliness of both Lockyers as they invited him into the room overlooking the river. They drank sherry with him and complimented him on the improvements he had made to the museum in such a short time. Lacey Lockyer even confided in him that not all of the museum committee had been in favour of the appointment of such a young man, and persuading them had not been easy. Then he became cautious at having revealed so much, and said, 'I am relying on your discretion not to repeat a word of this outside this room, Beamish, but I think I know my man.'

He did know his man. This was what caused Hugh such anguish when he confessed it afterwards, but at the time he enjoyed the flattery and failed to see where it was leading.

Nina Lockyer said, 'I'm so glad we can rely on you not to repeat confidences, Hugh, because it would never do if the *Messenger* got to know such things. Dreadful rumour-mongering rag.' And then she asked if he'd seen the report about King John's Lakes 'and that funny old man who lives there'.

Hugh laughed with her, but he thought he had better admit that the editor had asked him for some 'background stuff' on the Lakes.

Nina Lockyer was amused. 'Our dear Mr Puckeridge!' she exclaimed. 'What a horrid little man.'

'Typical of our dreadful press,' said her husband, 'although I happen to know that Mr Puckeridge isn't entirely to blame this time. I am told he was fed this particular rumour by one of his own reporters.' His eyes rested on Hugh.

'Really?' Hugh showed only slight interest. He was not about to betray Robin.

'A fellow called Horn.'

Hugh glanced away, but a silence developed that forced him to speak. 'Horn?' he said. 'I've met him.'

'How wonderful!' Nina Lockyer smiled at him. 'So you are right at the heart of Weldelph's secrets.'

'Hardly that,' said Hugh, but Nina Lockyer was not to be put off so easily. She leant forward until her perfume reached him.

'I would just love to know how newspapermen work, Hugh,' she smiled. 'For instance, where did your friend pick up his story in the first place?'

'I'm afraid I don't know, Mrs Lockyer.'

'How formal we are becoming! Please call me Nina—and allow me to fill your glass, Hugh.'

He was relieved that her questioning had eased off, and Lacey Lockyer himself appeared to kill the subject completely. Why should any of them, he asked, trouble themselves over the source of a reporter's lies? His wife pouted prettily but changed the subject.

'Tell me, Hugh, who else do you know in Weldelph? Any nice girls?' She became roguish. 'I'm quite sure you know some girls, Hugh.'

'I've hardly had time.'

'But now I know you're telling fibs!' She was triumphant. 'I've seen you with somebody—and a very pretty somebody at that.'

'I can't think who,' he said, but once again he felt a qualm.

'I saw her with you, in your car. You drove past this very window.'

He pretended to be puzzled for a moment, and then said, 'Oh that. She's just a girl who came to the museum with a query. I was helping her.'

'I even know her name, Hugh. Miss Charlotte Bush.'

'I'd quite forgotten,' he lied, but the subject was not allowed to drop.

'Bush?' said Lacey Lockyer. 'Did you say Bush?'

'It was you who pointed her out to me, darling. An unfortunate girl—with a brother who's not all he should be.' Her eyes twinkled. 'So you had better take care, Hugh.'

'Her brother,' said Lacey Lockyer, 'is not such a reprobate as is generally thought.'

'But he *has* been to prison.'

'Maybe, maybe. But I am more concerned with his aftercare, and I'm afraid I have a very worried man on my hands. He is deeply concerned about his sister who is, after all, still a schoolgirl.'

'Yes, of course.' It was time for Hugh to demonstrate his innocence. 'It was in connection with her school work that I came across her—she and her boyfriend, that is.' He breathed more easily. Boyfriend was the perfect smokescreen. 'They are at the same school,' he added.

'That is as may be.' The smooth face was turned towards him. 'But her brother has reason to think that there may be someone else in the background.' Lacey Lockyer paused. 'An older man.'

'Oh, Hugh,' Nina Lockyer cried, 'are you the one? Running around with a schoolgirl! What will the museum committee think?'

Hugh moved the muscles of his face but knew that his smile was not a success. 'I can assure you,' he began, but he could not curb Nina Lockyer's delight.

'Naughty Hugh! What will they do when they hear about you?'

'Nothing at all.' Once again it was Lacey Lockyer who came to the rescue. 'My committee will do nothing simply because they are going to hear nothing. I am not going to have a young man's career ruined by idle talk of him and a schoolgirl.'

Hugh opened his mouth but got no chance to speak.

'I was only joking, Lacey darling. Hugh's a good boy or he wouldn't be having drinks with the chairman, now would he?' She laughed lightly. 'A tête-à-tête with one of the most powerful men in Weldelph. Don't let him fool you, Hugh, he really pulls the strings.'

'Nina exaggerates.' The chairman's smile was warm, and Hugh was filled with gratitude. Lacey Lockyer, his protector, got to his feet and looked down on him benignly. 'I don't pull all the strings by any means. Take this trivial business of wishing to track down a silly rumour that has found its way into the paper. I am completely in the dark.'

'Who cares about old rumours?' Nina broke in. 'Hugh and I were talking about a lovely schoolgirl having an affair with someone who should know better, weren't we, Hugh?'

Her husband did not seem to have heard her. 'I would just like to know where that tale originated, that's all. A small point, of very little importance, yet it nags at one's brain.'

She ignored him. 'And right under our very noses, Hugh. Who on earth can she be carrying on with? Because Weldelph is a small place and there's bound to be trouble when it comes out—*if* it ever does, that is.'

'Rumours can poison a little community such as ours.' Lacey Lockyer fastened a button on his jacket. His smile remained, but a hint of coldness had come into his dark eyes. 'Rumours can, after all, ruin a man's reputation. Rumours should be traced, don't you think?'

'If it's possible.' Hugh longed to drink but found that he could not raise his glass to his lips.

'A man can be seriously damaged.' The museum chairman stood very still. 'Unless, of course, he has a measure of protection. Friends.'

Hugh fought to keep his gaze steady on Lacey Lockyer and succeeded. He would brazen it out. He had, after all, committed no crime. Then the chairman spoke again.

'Weldelph is your first curatorship, I understand, Mr Beamish. A very commendable first step in what should be a long career.'

Hugh said nothing. They knew. They certainly knew.

'Hugh?' There was a plaintive note in Nina Lockyer's voice and he turned towards her gratefully.

'Yes, Mrs Lockyer.'

'Please call me Nina.'

'I shall if you wish—if it's all right.' He was stumbling like a schoolboy when her voice came again, sweetly.

'Where did Mr Horn get his information, Hugh?'

'I really . . .' he began.

'Hugh,' she said, disappointed. Her husband began to walk towards the door. 'Are you leaving us, darling?' She raised her eyebrows at Hugh and spoke again just as Lacey Lockyer reached the door. 'We haven't offended you, have we, darling?'

There was no response, and Hugh panicked. Whatever else happened, he had to keep Lacey Lockyer talking.

'All I know,' he said, and Lacey Lockyer paused. 'All I know is that Robin Horn and I meet in a certain place.'

'A certain place?' Lacey Lockyer turned.

'We have a drink together.' Hugh licked his dry lips. That was not giving anything away. Everyone knew that journalists liked to drink. Robin certainly.

'A bar?'

Hugh nodded.

'A certain bar?'

He nodded again.

'And who else was in the bar?'

'Nobody.' He raised his eyes, willing the dark face to grasp the clue without him having to say another word.

152

If he said nothing there would be no treachery. 'Just Robin and me, and . . .' Their eyes held steady.

'And?' said the quiet man.

'Just Robin and me in the bar, and . . .'

'. . . and . . . and . . .' The dark eyes knew that the little word meant to tell him something. 'Ah . . . *and* the barman. Am I right, Hugh?'

Hugh shrugged.

'A particular barman?'

Hugh stared back.

'In a certain bar?'

Hugh looked away, and Nina Lockyer said, 'Such a devastatingly pretty girl. I wouldn't blame any man.'

Her husband was musing to himself. 'A certain elderly barman in a certain quiet bar. I do hope I am not mistaken.'

Hugh did not reply, and Lacey Lockyer went to the door and opened it for him.

'What a pity you must go,' said Nina Lockyer.

If he had decided at that moment to throw away his job and had savaged them both as hypocrites and blackmailers, Hugh could at least have saved some of his pride. What, in fact, he did was to pause and allow Nina Lockyer to say, 'I did so much want to know about the girl and the way she is behaving with an older man. However, I can only suppose it's natural when you consider her background, don't you agree, Hugh?'

For a split second, Hugh told my mother, his anger flared. But then it went out, quenched by cowardice. He nodded, and the consultant showed him the door.

'If only,' Hugh wrote, 'I had said something. If only . . . if only . . .'

By then it was too late.

27 Trigger and Virginia

It was what happened on Christmas Eve that made me realize I was close to the centre of a very strange story indeed. I could feel it in the air that morning. To begin with there was the silence of deep snow, and the sky brooded overhead with the promise of more snow to come. In the market place the stalls were roofed with thick white slabs, and paraffin lamps hissed and glared to make them into dragons' caves where apples and oranges were polished like wax and shone like heaps of impossible jewels. And there was the cold and the silence, and the three of us were waiting.

'Listen!' Virginia held up a hand. Somewhere, muffled by snow, a band was playing carols. 'It's a dream come true, Trigger. A white Christmas.'

'And the blasted owl, for all its feathers, was a-cold.' He stamped on snow packed hard by many feet. 'Damn it, Virginia, I'm freezing.'

'I think I'm beginning to like you, Trigger Harris, for your genuine Scroogeyness.'

'It's all that's left for a poor old man like me with a wizened heart.'

'What about me, then, Trigger? Who was it just now who saw the divine Charlotte trotting up the museum steps for moments of passion with her curator and entirely forgetting she had promised to meet us here? I called out but she didn't even turn her head. She's a minx; quite heartless.'

'What are you going to tell Harry?' I said. We were waiting for him as well as for Charlotte.

Virginia shrugged, but Trigger grinned and nodded

towards the corner of the square. Harry was stumbling towards us through the press of people.

'Trigger,' said Virginia, 'I warn you to be careful.'

He merely buried his thin red nose in his scarf, and did not lift it until Harry came near. Then he said, 'I don't wish to ruin your Christmas Eve drink with us, Harry my boy, but I doubt whether Charlotte is going to be present.'

'How come?'

'She's been seen elsewhere.'

Virginia's elbow caught Trigger as she leant in front of him to speak to Harry. 'Pay no attention to him,' she said. 'She'll be along later. I've just left her doing her Christmas shopping.'

'She's left it a bit late.' Harry looked around the square. 'Where was she?'

'At the museum, I believe,' said Trigger. 'Funny place to shop, but there you are.'

'She's not there now—and why don't you shut up, Trigger?' Virginia turned back to Harry. 'She was just coming out.'

'I wonder what she's been doing in Weldelph museum on Christmas Eve,' Trigger mused.

'Checking on something.' Virginia snatched at Trigger's arm and clung to it. 'I don't know what. Anyway does it matter?'

It was Harry himself who answered. 'Oh yes it matters,' he said, 'and I don't think she's gone shopping.'

'My sentiments precisely,' said Trigger.

Whatever trouble Trigger had intended to cause misfired. Harry was grinning happily as he said, 'Shopping's got nothing to do with what Charlotte is up to. It's much more exciting than that.'

'And you don't mind?' Trigger's voice was almost a squeak.

'Why should I? Charlotte and I have been working on

155

something together and that's why she's been to see Hugh Beamish, I expect.'

If I had asked him what was happening, he would probably have told me about the grasshopper, but I was distracted by Virginia. She glared at Trigger, warning him not to ask about Hugh Beamish, and for once the mischief was too great even for him. He remained snide, however. 'I hope all three of you will be very happy,' he said.

'We will.' Harry was so innocent it was painful to watch. 'If she's left the museum,' he said, 'I think I know where I can find her.'

He began to move away, but Virginia tried to prevent him. Wherever he was headed, he would not find Charlotte there. 'Don't go,' she pleaded. 'You promised to have a drink with us, Harry.'

'Have one for both of us.' He began to thread his way among the shoppers. He waved and called out, 'Merry Christmas!'

'Bah!' said Trigger. 'Humbug!'

Virginia turned on him. 'You're an absolute beast!' But her attitude was already changing, and I saw her cling tighter to his arm. 'I think I love you,' she said.

'That's not going to make me buy you a drink, Virginia.'

'Come on.' She tugged him. 'We can perhaps knock down a carol singer on the way.'

'Virginia's herself again,' he said.

I saw Harry turn as he left the square. He could see that the other two were laughing, and he waved again. He was relieved to see that he had not offended any of us, and he was happy because he was sure he knew where Charlotte had been heading when she was last seen. She was probably at the Lakes already.

He was mistaken. Charlotte was at home.

28 Betrayed

'What you so pale for, little sister?' said Derek. 'You should have nice rosy cheeks like a robin, all ready for tomorrow.'

Charlotte said nothing.

'Her,' said her mother. 'It's not a bit of use talking to her. She won't even put that bit o' holly over the pictures though I've asked her twenty times if I've asked her once. Merry bloody Christmas we're going to have tomorrow with her lookin' like that.'

Charlotte was sitting by the fire with a newspaper in her lap. She folded it slowly and put it down beside her chair. 'Where is it, then?' she said. 'I'll get it done now.'

'Out back where I left it.' Her mother rummaged in the drawer of the telly table and pulled out a pair of scissors. 'You'll need something to cut it up with.'

Derek tried to keep the peace. 'Mother's right,' he said, 'we don't actually want the pictures weighted down by great lumps of holly like blasted *tree* trunks.'

'You'll be lucky,' said his mother, 'there ain't a fat lot.'

Charlotte took the scissors, but Derek levered himself from his chair and said, 'I'll give you a hand, Lottie. You don't hardly look as if you got the strength.'

The condescension in his voice made her temper snap. She hurled the scissors to the floor. 'Do it your bloody self!' she yelled and stood, white-faced, glaring at him.

Her mother, round-shouldered, looked from one to the other, and then her voice came, sharp and vicious.

'Hit her, Derek!' she said. 'Give her one!'

But Derek drew deeply on his cigarette and shook his head as smoke seeped from his nostrils. 'That ain't

157

hardly appropriate, Mother, at this season o' the year. Especially as we're all here together in the family home, thankfully. Christmas, in all its essentials, is a family time, after all.'

'Oh, Christ!' Charlotte barged past the table and into the kitchen. She slammed the door and stood against the sink, pressing her stomach on the cold rim. If Hugh Beamish had only left a word. A single word. A word written down. 'I was smiling,' she said aloud. 'I was smiling.'

It came again, the shameful smile at Mrs Frost as she asked to see Mr Beamish.

'He's not here.'

'I'll wait, then.' Still smiling.

'He won't be back till after the holiday.' He had put a case in his car, said Mrs Frost. He had gone. No, there was no message, no note. He would be back in the New Year.

The kitchen door behind her opened and closed. 'Well,' said Derek, 'what has my pretty little sister been up to? Cigarette?'

'Just give me a drag of yours.' She lifted Derek's hand holding the cigarette and inhaled. Then she stood back.

'If I got any understanding of female psychology,' he said, 'this is a spot o' boy trouble. There's a feller in it, am I right?'

'Might be.'

'I might a known it.' He watched her raise a hand to her cheek. 'When I see you wipe away a tear from the corner of one of them hazel eyes I just wonder who could've done such a thing to my own sister.'

'So do I.' She opened her eyes wide to prevent the tears spilling.

'He ain't going to get away with it, no matter what he done.'

'You don't have to worry, Derek. Nobody's done anything, anything at all.'

158

'Well, that's one good thing anyway.' He took a final drag and threw his cigarette butt into the sink, 'If you're not in any sort o' trouble. You mean it?'

She nodded. Not in trouble. Not pregnant on Christmas Eve. No, nothing like that. 'Derek,' she said, and he waited. 'I smashed a Napoleon teacup. It was worth a lot of money.'

'I'm not quite wi' you.'

'I did it because he told me to. He wanted me to do it.'

'Well, you got to make him pay. If he was the party responsible then you got to make him pay. That's the law. You ain't got to pay a penny.'

She looked at him. 'You like money, don't you, Derek?'

'I can take it or leave it. I generally leave it. That's my philosophy of life, and look where it got me.'

'In a grotty kitchen on Christmas Eve,' she said. 'Me an' all.'

It was a long time since they had talked together, and longer since they had smiled at each other. 'Why do you always wear a scarf indoors?' she asked.

He looked down at the tasselled ends that lay on the bulge of his pullover. 'In case a boat goes over a weir,' he said. 'I could dangle me scarf from the bridge and the people could hang on. I been thinking about rescues ever since I was a boy.'

'Oh, damn it, Derek,' she said.

He looked up and saw the tears running down her face. He did not move except to take out another cigarette and light it while he gazed at her steadily. 'I seen girls in your sort o' state before, Lottie. It's more or less normal, so there's nothing to worry about.'

'Thank you very much!' Anger showed in her swimming eyes, and he patted the air with his cigarette hand to calm her.

'Hormones,' he said. 'It's a hormonium reaction, and what you need is taking out o' yourself.' He paused, and then he said, 'I seen something that might end your problem.'

He stood where he was, watching her struggle not to sob.

'I been keeping an eye on a certain old gentleman, Lottie, who lives down King John's Lakes.' When she nodded he went on, 'I been doing it in a kindly sense because a client of mine wants to do him a good turn in an underhanded way, if you follow me. Well, I done it to the best of my ability, but I didn't bargain for what I seen down there.' His eyes were on her, waiting. 'In the barn.'

He remained silent so long that eventually she nodded and managed to mutter a word. 'Grasshopper,' she said.

'You're wi' me!' He had struck a match, uselessly, and now he blew it out. 'There can't be many of that sort of thing around, Lottie, can there?' She shook her head. 'That could be very unique, that insect, and I was wondering, that when old Josh Lovegrove moves on ... I mean he wouldn't want to take it with him, would he?'

'Mr Lovegrove's all right. He's not going to die or anything.'

Her brother laughed. ''Course he ain't, Lottie. I was just wondering what was going to happen to it because there's a big demand for antique articles of that nature, and I was wondering if I could put in a bid, enter into a private negotiation before them sharks get their teeth into the poor helpless old sod. Are you wi' me?'

'No,' she said. 'I'm not.'

'Well, I do know my little sister have been fornicating around down there, so I thought she might put in a word with the old gentleman on behalf of her brother.'

'Why should I, Derek?' She was bewildered. 'He's not going to sell it. He's got no reason to.'

'Not going to sell? Ain't you seen today's paper, Lottie?'

160

The kitchen door opened and her mother came half way into the kitchen. She had been listening. 'She ain't got eyes for anything like that, Derek. She ain't got eyes for anything that'd help her brother.'

'Mother, we come out here to cut some holly, am I right?' The interruption had exasperated him. 'We come out here privately to cut some bloody leaves and bloody berries to look nice behind the bloody picture frames. Do that sound reasonable to you?'

'Stuck up little cow. You'll get nothing out of her.'

'I don't want nothing out of her, Mother. I just want her to put in a word for me now old Josh Lovegrove is going to sell up and go. That's all, Mother. While we was hacking the bloody holly into tiny pieces I just wanted a word with her.'

Charlotte said, 'I didn't know old Josh was leaving.'

'You was reading the paper,' said her mother. 'It was all in there. What was your mind on? Which one of them fellers you was going to let maul you next?'

'That was slightly uncalled for, Mother,' said Derek.

'What d'you know about it? You can't tell me she don't flaunt it around where it do her the most good. I seen the dirty little cat. I know her!' She lifted a thin hand and pointed, but Derek held her wrist and led her back into the living room.

Charlotte heard their voices and could take no more. Her coat hung at the back of the kitchen door. She put it on and went out.

29 Christmas Eve

There's a great conspiracy to make Christmas Eve different from the rest of the year. It seeps into every detail. I was aware of it as I was wrapping presents, tying them up with golden string and sticking on Christmas seals, each one of them like a secret window showing Christmas ready to come in—tiny snowmen grinning on starlight nights, stage coaches and inns with their doors wide to let light stream out onto the snow, and carol singers grouped around lanterns with their little black dots of mouths wide open and singing. And all of them in the snow, generally in the depths of the night. They took my mind outside, and I thought of the market stalls, all dark now, with scraps of paper freezing to the bare planks where the fruit had shone like Christmas tree baubles.

Harry was out there. He was standing on the bridge as the last of the shops closed. In the river, rafts of frozen snow, like ghostly lily pads, rotated slowly and he watched their soft edges crumble as they were crushed together by the tide.

He knew now he had been wrong about Charlotte. She had not been to the Lakes, but he had stayed there, working feverishly alongside Josh to keep her out of his mind. Nothing had gone right. He watched the grey lily pads as they overlapped in reluctant matings beneath the bridge, and the long afternoon of failure pressed in on him.

The grasshopper did not work. He knew now it never would. All afternoon he had laboured with Josh to complete the stringing of the American Gut, but by the time the sun had gone down and they were working by lamplight to finish hooking and stretching the gut within the creature's entrails, it was obvious that they had put no strength into its limbs. No matter how often they restrung the gut or how hard they tautened it, the legs would splay weakly the instant they tried to move it, and it would collapse. It had a saddle of velvet, but he had never for a moment succeeded in riding it. The grasshopper was lifeless.

What made it even worse was that his father had seen

162

him and Josh at work. Julian Green had laughed and humoured them like a couple of children.

Harry swung his head up to shake the memory out of his mind. The housefronts along The Sweep were dark, but at that moment someone pushed a curtain to one side and made an upward pointing dagger of yellow light.

'Come and join me, darling.' Even long afterwards when she had to describe the scene, Nina Lockyer could recall the words she used as she stood in the window, looking out. 'Bring your glass.'

Harry saw the silhouettes of two people in the thickest part of the dagger.

'You may put your arm around me, darling. There's no one to see.'

But there was someone to see, and eventually to hear. People with secrets should not breathe them on Christmas Eve.

Harry saw Lacey Lockyer put his arm around his wife, and they held the pose with the glow of the room behind them.

'I love Christmas,' she said. 'We are so lucky, you and me.'

Luck, he said, played no part; even on Christmas Eve he had been busy. He did not tell her what had been occupying him for most of the day, and she did not ask. Instead, she turned towards him and kissed him.

Harry saw the curtain fall back into place, and he looked away upstream. Beyond the shadow of the bridge the ice floes opened their faces to the moon and blossomed into grey chrysanthemums painted on a Japanese box. The moon was carefully placed in the lacquered sky.

Charlotte was also wandering in the night. If he had walked a hundred paces in the right direction he would have seen her in the telephone kiosk. She risked ringing his house for the last time.

163

'I'm sorry,' said his mother, 'he's still not home,' and then, failing to cover the mouthpiece properly, she spoke to someone in the room. 'It's that girl again—the one who wants to speak to Harry about that grass-hopper thing.'

Charlotte shut her eyes. The grasshopper had been her excuse for wanting to talk to him. She should never have mentioned it.

Then she heard another voice, his father's: 'Give it here. I'll put an end to this.' But Charlotte hung up.

There was an iron coldness in Harry's toes, but he could not yet go home. His father owned the Lakes. The sale was certain. Old Josh had signed the papers in the barn that afternoon when the fiasco of the grasshopper was at its worst. He had seen Harry sprawling in the tangle of its feeble legs, and he would be waiting for a chance to laugh again when he got home.

Harry walked to the end of the bridge. By the railings the snow was pitted where a dog had peed. He crossed the road. In the cold air high above the street a string of lights, yellow, blue, green and red, zig-zagged towards the empty market square. The brightness gave the illusion of warmth, but it was too steady, with none of the flickering life of flame, and beneath his feet the trodden snow crackled like pond ice.

Charlotte left the phone box, and her footsteps took her away from him.

30 To the Management

Lacey Lockyer had had a busy day talking to people. It is known that he spoke to the management of a Weldelph hotel, and he was seen shortly afterwards climbing the stairs to the editor's office of the Weldelph

Messenger, but the conversations took place behind closed doors and what was actually said has never come out into the open. The only certainty is that Lacey Lockyer was able to make use of what Hugh Beamish had revealed about a barman who listened and a reporter who spoke out. And those two found out about it because Lacey Lockyer knew how to draw blood.

My mother and father saw the result of his day's work and were still talking about it when they came home from the Horse and Groom that night. They always do go out on Christmas Eve, and I don't mind because I can spread myself wrapping up presents, and anyway they're quite fun when they get back. The festivities get under way. This time they had plenty to talk about, and I must say my father is quite good at imitating the way a drunk talks—which he had to do when he described hearing the barman. George (and my father had to do the same) took great care with his enunciation when he said, 'I was labouring under the misapprehension, Mr Horn, that you were going home for Christmas. Wherever that should be, naturally— home, that is.'

'There will be time for that on the morrow, old son,' said Robin Horn. 'Plenty of time. All the time in the world. Time enough.' He also took pains to speak clearly.

The bar, on this night of the year, was crowded. My mother was sure that the decorations could never have changed in George's time. There were some rich but decomposing red and green loops across the ceiling and a gilded card that muttered Season's Greetings among the glasses behind the whisky optics. George had his waistcoat tightly buttoned and armbands around his shirtsleeves. He was girded for business but served no one. He had an assistant, a young man with neat hair, great politeness and such a rapid hand at the pumps that he appeared to need no help from George. He got none.

With the counter between them, Robin and George leant against the wall at the end of the bar. Robin nodded towards the assistant. 'You've got to admit it, George, he's an efficient young bugger.'

'Management trainee, Mr Horn. The cream of the cream.'

'And abstemious with it. He hasn't had a drink all evening.'

'A lily-livered little milksop, sir. I won't have a word said against him.'

My father was very amused, but my mother was watching Robin, who had slumped with both elbows on the bar. He suddenly straightened and looked across the room. 'By George, George, it's thick in here.'

'Ho, ho, sir.'

'I don't know why you sir me, George, when I've just got you the sack.'

'Not you, Mr Horn. *You* are not the snake in the grass who broke the seal of confidence. It must have been the museum gentleman who divulged. Permit me to draw you another pint.'

My mother and father were all ears, but they didn't like to butt in when somebody had just got the sack. They had another surprise coming.

Robin rolled his head and squinted at the barman. 'I'll have a pint just as long as you're having a modicum yourself, George.'

'I am indeed. I am in festive mood.' George waved the assistant away from the pumps, drew a pint, poured his own colourless liquid, ignored a customer and did not approach the cash register. Then he raised his glass. 'To the management.'

'To the management.' Robin put down his glass. 'What was I saying?'

'You were saying we were both in the same boat, Mr Horn. The management has dispensed with our services.'

166

'You've hit it on the button, George. They were the Puke's very words.'

'Similarly with me, Mr Horn, as voiced by my manager, God rest his soul.'

'And so, George, you said to him . . .'

'I thanked his nibs for having the best interests of his staff at heart and informed him that I had never worked for a better lickspittle or fartcatcher than himself and trusted that *his* master would be pleased. But I am a little hurt, Mr Horn, as I invited him for a farewell drink tonight but he has not put in an appearance.'

'Discourteous, George.'

'Modern manners, Mr Horn. May I ask what you said to Mr Puckeridge at the parting of the ways?'

'Not a word, George. His desk fell over.'

'Dear me.'

'And I left to get help immediately because it had pinned him to the floor. It was a nasty shock. May I buy you a drink?'

'Certainly, sir.'

Glasses were filled without money changing hands. My parents' eyebrows had gone up and stayed up.

'To the management, Mr Horn.'

'To the management, George.'

They surveyed the crowded scene through the haze.

'Quite a seasonal gathering, Mr Horn.'

'But after tonight, George old mate, what's to become of you?'

'You don't have to worry on my account. I have a cosy little billet with the old friend I was telling you about. Drink up, Mr Horn, it's my shout.'

'To the management.'

'To the management, sir, and coupling with it a certain insect.'

They put their glasses down and, with their hands on the counter as though a confrontation was taking place, they gazed long and steadily at each other.

167

'I'm glad you reminded me of that, George.'

'It's a very rare creature, Mr Horn. It needs protection.'

'And who better to protect it than Weldelph's most notable benefactors?'

'I would like to take wine,' said the barman, raising his glass, 'with Mr Julian Green.'

'And I,' said Robin, 'with Mr Lacey Lockyer.'

They clinked glasses. 'The benefactors!' they said.

My parents were mystified, especially about the reference to an insect.

31 Gone Midnight

Two people had been sacked, so I knew something was stirring that night, but even if I had guessed that the grasshopper was going to play a part on Christmas Eve, I would never have got within a mile of what actually happened. It was an even greater surprise to Harry.

When he eventually got home he found a note propped against the coffee jar on the kitchen table alongside a mug and a plate with a sandwich wrapped in cling film. The note said: 'Left the Christmas lights on for you. Switch them off before you go to bed.' Then his mother had printed in large letters 'MERRY XMAS', but underneath, in small handwriting, almost secretively, she had written: 'Where have you been? A *girl* has been ringing you up about an insect!!!'

Harry bent over, reading it as he began to unzip his windcheater. His fingers were stiff, his nose and ears were numb, and now that he was in the warmth of the kitchen he was aware that his jeans were harsh and cold against his legs.

The message was a thread attached to *girl*, and then it

was an invisible filament leading out to the streets of Weldelph, to the blank face of the dark museum where he had watched for her, to the black, trodden ice of Scrapeshin's Passage where icicles made a dragon's snarl of the café's empty window, and to Trigger's house and Virginia's where he had been invited in, and at last to her own house where, at the door, her mother had told him Charlotte had gone out, she didn't know where. The thread ran everywhere and back to the tiny knot in his mother's scribble, *girl*.

His fingers slowed on the zip. By seeking her, he had lost her. Time after time she must have vanished around a corner just as he came into a street, or he had doubled back when he would have found her by merely going ahead. He saw their figures as they had flitted from place to place seeking each other—when it was not movement that they had needed, but lack of movement. If one of them had remained still they would have come together. Now it was too late. Doors were locked and lights had been put out.

The notches of the zip clicked slower under his fingers. Outside, the moon was on the snow. There must be a trace of her out there, somewhere she had left a mark. He could still seek her, like a dog with the scent of her in his muzzle. The zip slid unsteadily. If it got to the end without jamming, and if his jacket fell open, then he would remain where he was. His fingers would decide.

There was one place that, if she had rested there, he would be certain to find a trace. His hand twisted and the zip faltered. It would be useless. He would be heading in the wrong direction when by now she was at home and in bed. Useless.

Without his mind having anything to do with it, his fingers moved upwards and closed his jacket.

He put the sandwich in his pocket, replaced the coffee jar on its shelf, and put the mug beside the sink as though it had been used. He switched off all the lights, eased the outer door open against the crack of the ice, and went out.

Gone midnight. He slipped on the path and almost fell. The front gate creaked, frozen and unwilling to be disturbed, and he moved away quickly in case the sound should bring eyes to windows. He was the only traveller and he walked quickly until the houses, like black gnomes hooded in snow, were hidden by the white weight of the trees, and the town was behind him. He was in the domain of the moonlight and winter. The snow in the lane gave muffled grunts as he trudged through its thick pelt, but the sound of each footstep died and left no ripple in the silence that closed over him.

It was the dead of night. In the town at his back no paper wrappings yet rustled or torches secretly picked out the shapes of packages heaped in bedrooms. Only pigeons, stirring as the coldness shifted to gain a tighter grip on roofs and church towers, blinked in their dark nooks and looked out on what Harry could see as the lane climbed a low bank.

The Lakes had gone. The landscape had been swept smooth by tide after tide of snow until only the shadows of hedges, like the ribs of ancient wrecks, broke the whiteness. He paused and became part of the silence. It was at that moment, but as though it had always been there, as unheard as the sigh of the open sky, that a sound reached him. It came from far away, a cry like the thin yell that a skater might make far out on the ice, or the shrill voices of children playing. Yet no earthly children would be playing so deep into the night. He listened, as motionless as a stump, his feet buried. It came again, like a bird's shriek over the wasteland. Then, cut suddenly short, it left the air empty.

He waited, but it did not come again and he began to run, stumbling where the drifts sloped from the hedges into the track. He would have missed the gate to the

170

Lakes if it had not been left jammed half open in the snow, and he was breathless when he rounded the last bend and saw the railway carriage beached on its white bank. It lay like a fat caterpillar with lights glowing in several of its segments and no blinds were drawn. The bell wire was frozen and his rap on the heavy door did not carry against the voices inside. He heaved at the door and stepped into the corridor, calling out Josh's name as he did so. There was no answer, and he let the door thud shut.

'Didn't,' said a man's voice, then repeated itself. 'Didn't look real to me, not for a minute.' Pause and repeat. 'Not for a minute did I believe any of it, especially when . . . dear oh lor', that I'll never believe.'

Harry called out again and stamped snow from his boots, but the voices were at the far end of the corridor and too intent on what they were saying to be interrupted. He spoke Josh Lovegrove's name again, but only as a token, too quietly to be overheard. Then he listened.

The same voice came again. 'Looked like . . . looked like something that had just stepped off the top of a Christmas tree. That's what she looked like to me.'

The next voice was quieter but unmistakable. 'A very pretty fig-you-are indeed.'

Then a girl's laughter. 'I'm no Christmas tree fairy. My bottom's too big.'

Harry shut his eyes. He had found her where no one but himself would think to look. At Christmas.

Josh's voice. 'You must be frozen, Miss Bush. Put this around your shoulduars.'

There was a shuffling sound and she thanked him. Harry should have moved forward then, but he wanted to hear more. Christmas Eve did not disappoint him.

'I just wish he'd been there when it happened,' she said. 'He's had much more to do with it than me. He deserved to see it.'

'There will be a time, Miss Bush. All is not lost.'

171

'But tonight, Josh. It should have been tonight. I've been horrible to him, I really have, in lots of ways you don't know about. Nobody does.'

'You tried, Miss Bush. You tried to let him know. Come closer to the fire, you're shivering.'

'It was so bright out there,' she said. 'Bright enough to see where I was going no matter how fast I went. But it was cold.'

'Then allow me.' The first voice came again, and Harry moved further along the corridor until he could see an angle of the compartment. The man's back moved across it. He saw shirtsleeves, the satin back of a waistcoat, a thick neck and grey hair cut short and oiled flat. He heard a liquid poured. 'Just a sip, young woman. It always works.'

The satin back lurched slightly, and Josh said, 'Not so much, George. Young ladies do not have your capacity. You must treat her like your daught-you-are.'

'It burns!' Charlotte was gasping.

'I said a sip!' cried George. 'Gulp it like that and you will be as drunk as I am.'

'I think I'm drunk already. I feel drunk. I must have been drunk to do what I did.'

George spoke solemnly. 'Young woman, no matter what anybody else may think of you, you have made two old men feel young again this night. And your secret is safe with us, am I not right, old partner?'

Josh Lovegrove must have nodded because George went on, 'There's a mint of money in that machine o' yours, Josh. There will be, when it catches on. You never had no need to sell up, and I never had no need to get myself the sack. We could be sitting pretty.' He gave a thick chuckle, and roguery came into his voice. 'I'm not maintaining we could sit as pretty as you sit, Miss Bush—but pretty pretty, never you mind.'

'Now you're being rude, George,' she said, teasing him.

172

'I could get ruder. I'm in the mood.'

Josh cut across their laughter. 'It took a young lady to make my Uncle Cox's dream come true.'

'And Harry,' she said. 'Don't forget the American Gut. He found it for you. He wanted to make it work more than me. I didn't believe in it.'

'The secret,' said Josh, 'is so simple and so difficult it took a young maiden to find it.'

'I didn't know what I was doing. I was so miserable I let it happen. Do you think I dare show him, Josh? I may not be able to do it in daylight. What if I forget? What if it all leaves me?'

'Hark?' George's bark silenced them. 'I heard a sound!'

Harry reached back and fumbled the door open. 'Are you there, Josh?' he called and slammed it shut.

'And who might you be?' The red face and heavy moustache glared at him from the doorway. 'This is a private party.' But Josh was small enough to wriggle past George and into the corridor where he grasped Harry by the arm.

'Christmas is complete!' Old Josh's face was bright. His eyes and his bristles sparkled. 'Dark deeds and great magic.'

'Is Charlotte there?' Harry kept up the pretence. 'I got a message and I thought she might be.' And then he saw her sitting by the stove, an old grey blanket around her shoulders and a glass in her hand. 'You rang me,' he said.

'Sorry.' She pulled the blanket closer and blushed. Then she shook her hair free of the blanket and it lay on her shoulder. 'I didn't mean to drag you out here in the middle of the night. You've got your family, and everything. They'll worry.'

'They don't know I'm here.'

'Oh.' She dipped her head and looked away from him. 'That's all right then.'

173

There was silence and he felt the eyes of the two old men on him. 'No, it's not all right.' He turned to Josh. 'Why did you sell the Lakes, Mr Lovegrove?'

Josh was smiling. 'No one can live for ever, young man. And this is too much space for one man.'

'He'll turn you out.'

'He might, and he might not. Why concern yourself about such a trivial mattuar?'

Trivial. How could it be trivial? Harry opened his mouth but no words came.

'It has gone midnight,' said the little man, 'and the secret is known. The maiden has tamed the unicorn.' He stood back and smiled and waited until Charlotte lifted her face and looked at him. 'Are you going to show him?'

'I wouldn't dare,' she said. 'Not like this. Not now.'

'It is dark,' said Josh.

'There's a moon.'

'Moonlight is a state of nature.' He motioned for George to sit down and at the same time held open the door to the corridor. 'We shall wait here.'

Harry saw her hesitate, but then she stood up quickly and swept past without looking at him. Nothing was said and he followed her out into the freezing air. Her blanket made a black cloak that swept the snow. 'You needn't worry about Josh,' she said. 'He doesn't mind about selling the Lakes. The grasshopper was the only thing that interested him. And I don't think he cares about that any more.'

'Why not? I don't understand.'

She shrugged. 'Because somebody has ridden it, I suppose. He's proved his point. The rest doesn't matter.'

Still he did not understand but he sensed that she did not wish to be pressed. 'You've made a hit with those two old fellers,' he said.

She laughed. 'Any girl can do that. With any man. At any time.'

'No, I don't mean that, Charlotte. They like you.'

'Any girl,' she said again. 'Any time. Provided she can do what I did.'

He was swinging his head towards her to ask a new question when he saw the grasshopper. It had no colour now except blackness. And it stood clear of the barn, out on the lake. Its shape was drawn on the whiteness like part of a spindly thicket denuded of its leaves by winter.

'You left it out there,' he accused her. 'On the ice.'

'The old gents wanted to see me ride it once more. They think it's magic.'

'Maybe it is.' The words came in small clouds from his lips.

'We'll see about that.'

They walked side by side through the snow. 'How did you get it out here?' he asked. 'It's heavy.'

Her laughter was a strange sound under the moon. 'It walked,' she said. 'It walks for me. Look.'

They had approached to within a few paces, and now she went ahead, reached up and touched the grass-hopper's head. It nodded so that the moon slid in its eyes and she tugged gently at its bridle and spoke. 'Come on, my lovely man. Follow me.'

Somewhere within it the pendulum must have been rocked, and the rocking must have transferred itself to the sinews of gut, but Harry heard nothing of that. The only sound was made by the claw of a single leg as it broke clear of the crust of snow.

'Look out!' Harry darted back as the knee joint of one of its huge hind legs angled itself higher against the sky and then the foot scraped forward, drawing a furrow in the snow. It was levering itself forward, stalking her as she went ahead, ready to leap. It was a gigantic skeleton that would crush her.

'Charlotte!'

She turned her head, laughing over her shoulder as

she walked forward, and the long lozenge of the creature's body lurched behind her. She manoeuvred it to face the moon, and stopped.

'You're not afraid of it, are you, Harry?'

'I don't know.' All afternoon he had tried to make it work for him, but its feeble legs had buckled and it had collapsed like a puppet. 'What have you done to it?'

'Nothing. Would you like to ride it?'

'If you show me how.'

'Nobody showed me. You heard what Josh said—it'll do what it's supposed to do if you don't think about it.'

'But I've never ridden a grasshopper.'

'Don't think about it. Just be natural. I was.'

'I don't know what natural means.'

'You'll never find out by thinking about it. Just do it.'

She handed him the bridle and he took it and put his other hand to the joint of the foreleg. The two parts of the joint fitted so close, one part folded around the other, that his fingers could detect no hinge. It was as cold as ice.

'Hold its head still,' he said, for its short antennae, dipping with its nodding head, seemed to be responding to a faint tremble he could detect within its body. 'Hold its head!'

She put her hand to its muzzle, and when she had steadied it Harry raised one foot to its upper leg where it straddled the snow, hoisted himself up, put his leg over its back and eased himself into the curve of its soft saddle. He sat above her, looking down. 'What now, Charlotte?'

'It belongs to you, Harry.' She released its head. 'Ride it.'

The whole beast trembled and the head dipped away from him. 'I'm falling!' he cried.

She stepped back without a word and he reached forward, grabbing at the horns to steady the dipping

176

head. The saddle tilted with him. He twisted and caught a glimpse of back legs folding. They would swing like scythes. They must be stilled. He hauled back, and the long, segmented body went back with him, sloping down until it settled on its haunches. Mastery. He let out his breath slowly and held himself and his creature motionless while he worked out what to do next. He turned to look over his shoulder just as her cry reached him.

'Don't look back! Don't think! Ride!'

But think he must. And he had to see what was happening. It was necessary, or there could be no control. He let the head ease forward, keeping watch as he did so. Weight shifted under his saddle. He felt it sliding, and as it fell away there was the throb of something under tension, straining to be free. He fought to contain it, clutching tight at the head, burning with hatred at the bulging eyes that looked back at him with their white moon specks, detesting the mechanical insect that would not obey.

'Damn you!' The words were in his teeth as he wrestled, driving feet into its sides, forcing it down. There was a moment of stillness, of victory, and he let his head fall until his chin was on his chest.

At that moment it leapt. Whatever power his struggle had put into it was, in the shudder of an instant, released. There was a clang of metal against metal and a thrash of limbs. Then a strange silence and lightness as he and the grasshopper were flung upwards. They had left the ground and its back was vertical, pointing to the sky. He parted from it, sliding backwards, losing his grip, cradled for a moment in the free air before he fell and hit the snow. His bones were jarred and his eyes were shut. He put his arms over his face and curled up, fearing that the flailing limbs would stab him when they came down.

'Harry!'

177

He heard her voice but was still afraid to look.

'Harry!'

He uncurled to see her standing above him, and the great head of the beast behind her.

'You didn't give yourself a chance, Harry. You're not being yourself at all.'

He raised himself on one elbow. 'Show me,' he said. 'What do I have to do?'

'Nothing much,' she said. 'Just forget everything— everything you've been taught. Just forget.'

'I don't know what you mean.' His head fell forward and he was looking at the edge of her blanket cloak. There was something strange, something he had not noticed. 'Your feet,' he said. 'You've got no shoes.' He saw her toes in the trampled snow. 'Why are your feet bare?'

He raised his eyes to her face as she looked down.

'Why?' he said. 'I don't understand.'

The shadow made by her lips smiled down at him. 'Who needs shoes for riding grasshoppers, Harry?'

She was still smiling as she parted her cloak and let it fall. She shed it in the moonlight and stood naked in the snow.

'It's a question,' she said, 'of balance.' The moonlight made snow of her shoulders and breasts. Her belly was smooth and dimpled and shadowed where it reached the valley of her thighs. 'Let me show you.'

She stepped away from him and in a moment was astride the grasshopper's back, cleaving to it. Two old men had seen her do that. Unclothed. Herself and nothing else in the moonlight.

She rocked in the icy air, and the grasshopper's legs began to prod the snow, ungainly at first but then, as she coaxed, the mechanical animal obeyed, turned and gathered itself and leapt. It vanished. He lost sight of it against the blackness of the sky. Then far away a shadow disturbed the snow, but only for an instant as

178

Charlotte and the beast rocked and launched themselves again.

Her cry reached him, like the shriek of a hunting owl or a child playing, far away and out of reach.

PART SIX

32 The Moth

The facts are never enough. You have to use your imagination to get at the truth. Charlotte knew the facts and told Virginia, so that by the time the story got to me I did not have to use very much imagination to know it all. But one evening, just to check, I took a walk along the riverbank and there was the old Cortina exactly where they said it would be. Derek and the milkman were inside, and their lips were moving.

'You never told me,' said the milkman, 'that the exhaust was going to drop off.'

'What time of the year is it?' Derek looked up into the car's roof where there was a small tear in the fabric covering. He wetted a finger and ran it along the split, pressing hard. It did nothing to heal it. 'Come on, Ted, what part of the year are we in?'

'Spring,' said Ted, 'but I don't see what that's got to do with my exhaust.'

'And what have you noticed about springtime from your point of view as a motorist?'

'It's wet, and the rain ain't all outside the bodywork.'

'No, Ted, no. What have you noticed about the roads apart from the wet? I mean scattered about everywhere, lying in the gutters and on the verges, practically in heaps in some places?'

'Doggy-do's,' said Ted.

'Old exhaust pipes, Ted. Silencers. Rusted metal. Bits and pieces what've fallen off the underparts.'

'Car droppings,' said the milkman.

'Exactly, Ted.'

'No, I've never noticed.'

Derek sighed. 'You've heard of the Fall, Ted? I'm not referring to it in the biblical sense of Adam and Eve and all that stuff about original sin. None o' that, and not the bloody leaves coming off the trees in autumn. The Fall, Ted, is a technical term in the motor trade and refers specifically to what happens after all that salt has got under your car in the winter months. Exhausts drop off.'

'Original tin.' The milkman looked straight ahead. 'What I want to know, Derek, is what we're doing parked in this layby in the wet with the night comin' on. It's not as if you're still spying for Mr Lockyer. That's been knocked on the head.'

'Pride, Ted. It's a matter of self-respect. If I start something I see it through to the bitter end.'

'You generally have to,' said Ted. 'They don't let you out till you done your time.'

'Ted, Ted.' Derek shook his head. 'There wasn't any call for a remark like that.'

'I didn't want to offend you, Derek.'

'No offence taken, Ted.'

'I just thought I better tell you that if you've got a job in mind and you get done and sent to Norwich again I ain't comin' on visitors' day. I don't think this motor would make it. Not since the Fall.'

'I got nothing in mind, Ted. It's just a watching brief on my own account. As a matter of fact, Mr Lacey Lockyer was well satisfied with my services and gave me quite a sizeable bonus at Christmas time.'

'I know. I seen you lashin' out.'

'Sarcasm is not in order, Ted. The settlement was mutually satisfactory but not all that great in real terms. Which was why I took out that bit of insurance.'

'And which is on my premises at the moment.'

Derek licked his finger and again pressed the fabric.

182

'The wife could mend that with a needle and cotton in no time.'

'She might if you'd stop puttin' spit on it.'

'It's amazing, Ted, the way fate plays a hand. Who'd have thought an insect could have caused such an upset for Mr Lacey Lockyer?'

'He was pretty angry about that grasshopper, was he, when he found it missing?'

'No, Ted, not *that* insect. I mean the real thing, them little rare moths that live in King John's Lakes. They're a natural heritage, that's what they are, Ted, and they don't breed nowhere else so they got to be conserved, ain't they?'

'Oh, yes,' said Ted. 'Moths need lookin' after. I wouldn't like to see them droppin' down in heaps like car exhausts.'

'Nor would I, Ted. Nor would anybody.'

'Except Mr Lacey Lockyer who can't do nothing with the Lakes now they got the moth.'

'And his partner, Ted. Mr Julian Green was pretty angry when he heard the Lakes was to be protected for the moths and that nobody could do nothing to disturb them. Particularly not build marinas.'

'He give the game away, didn't he?' said Ted. 'He got so angry about the moths that he let it slip he had a partner. I wouldn't mind a bet he's sorry he done that.'

'Big court case now, Ted. Corruption in high places. And all because of a little tiny moth.'

'The *Messenger* done a good job, bringin' all that out.'

Derek looked at him with pity. 'You got a lot to learn about the ways of the world in Weldelph, Ted, if you think the *Messenger* had anything to do with it. I happen to have heard it from my contacts.'

'Ear at the keyhole.'

'No need for that, Ted. As you know, I'm not sneaky or dishonest in any way whatsoever.'

183

'I know that,' said Ted. 'I bought a car from you, didn't I?'

'I got contacts in Mr Lacey Lockyer's office, ain't I?'

'You should have, the time you spend there.'

'One o' them girls don't get on too well with Lady Lockyer, as a matter of fact, and she told me there'd been a big row with Julian Green who was blaming someone who used to work for the *Messenger* for bringing the moth to the attention of the general public. He done it after he left the *Messenger* and got a job on one of the big papers. Then he spilled the beans about everything—moth an' all. Feller called Robin something.'

'So a little bird told 'em,' said the milkman.

'Have it your own way, Ted.'

There was silence in the car except for the rain rattling on the roof. Perched high on the lonely riverbank they could see across the speckled lakes to the black barn and railway carriage alongside it. 'They'll be clearing all that away, I expect,' said the milkman, 'to make room for the moths.'

'No, Ted, that's another thing. Them sheds is habitat. The moths need 'em and they ain't got to be shifted.'

'Old Josh looks like a bit of moths' habitat hisself.'

'Might as well be. They've appointed him warden, him and his old mate from the pub.'

'You know a lot,' said Ted.

'I got a kid sister, ain't I? And she's a friend of old Josh Lovegrove.'

'She wouldn't be a friend for long if old Josh knew what her big brother was up to.'

'Insurance, Ted. That's all it is. And she don't know anything about it.'

'She knows how to ride it, you tell me, which is more'n you do.'

'So she says, but I never seen her. She just come home Christmas morning with this tale about ridin' a bloody grasshopper all night, and I thought she'd been glue-sniffing or something. Well, you know what the younger generation's like, Ted.'

'Immoral.'

'For once, Ted, you got the right word. She's got no sense of what she *ought* to do, morally speaking. That young feller Green, he's mad on her, but she won't have nothing more to do with him. Even though he's loaded—or will be, one day.'

'You told me his old man was going bankrupt any minute.'

Derek looked sideways at him from the shiny folds of his cheeks. 'There's always something stacked away for them people. They don't go down the spout like you and me, Ted. They got something hid away, they always have, which is why my little sister is immoral not to think of her poor old mother who could use a bob or two in her old age.'

'You're right,' said the milkman. 'If she was moral she'd let young Green get his end away.'

'Hold on, Ted, that ain't what I said.'

'That's the obvious thing to do if she wants to be moral. She's just letting it go to waste to keep it for herself.'

'Ted, will you wait, Ted.'

'She ought to share it around. Give and take.'

'Ted!'

'She's only the best-lookin' kid in the whole of bloody Weldelph so surely she can spare a bit for her family.'

'If you don't shut up, Ted, I'll get out of this car and walk home in the rain.'

'And see how I like that,' said Ted.

There was silence again while Derek lit a cigarette. He began speaking in a gout of smoke. 'She used to be keen on him, Ted, but all she says now is she feels sorry for him.'

'Me, too,' said the milkman. 'So near yet so far, poor young bugger.'

185

'Would have been different, she said, if he'd been able to ride that bloody grasshopper, but he couldn't. Couldn't free himself, she said, and be natural. What a load of old squit. She should never have ditched him for that. He ain't a bad-looking boy, so it wouldn't hardly be any sacrifice for her, and look at the fringe benefits.' He drew on his cigarette. 'There's only one good thing about it.'

'I thought there would be something,' said Ted.

'Well, it's an ill wind. Since my sister and that boy have split up neither of 'em has been down to the Lakes to ask about the grasshopper.'

'Wouldn't do 'em a lot of good if they did. Old Josh crated it up again.'

'In case of damage,' said Derek. 'I don't suppose he'll want to open it up for a long time.'

'He better not,' said the milkman, 'as it hopped away one night.'

'Insurance, Ted, that's all that was. It's quite safe where it is.'

'That's as maybe, but people are beginning to wonder why me car always stands outside the garage. Even in the wet.'

'Don't worry about it, Ted.'

'Specially when the exhaust keeps droppin' off.'

Derek sighed.